SO-AXP-078

ALAN AND THE
ANIMAL KINGDOM

Also by Isabelle Holland

OF LOVE AND DEATH AND OTHER JOURNEYS

HEADS YOU WIN, TAILS I LOSE

THE MAN WITHOUT A FACE

AMANDA'S CHOICE

CECILY

ALAN AND THE ANIMAL KINGDOM
by Isabelle Holland

J. B. Lippincott Company
Philadelphia and New York

U.S. LIBRARY OF CONGRESS CATALOGING IN PUBLICATION DATA

HOLLAND, ISABELLE.
  ALAN AND THE ANIMAL KINGDOM.

  SUMMARY: WHEN THE AUNT WHO IS HIS GUARDIAN DIES, AN OR-
PHANED BOY DECIDES TO TELL NO ONE AND SO MAKE SURE THAT HIS
COLLECTION OF PET ANIMALS WON'T BE DESTROYED WHEN HE IS SENT
TO A NEW HOME.
  [1. ANIMALS—FICTION. 2. ORPHANS—FICTION] I. TITLE.
PZ7.H7083Al   [FIC]   76–55371
ISBN–0–397–31745–X

FOR JOAN KAVANAUGH

ALAN AND THE ANIMAL KINGDOM

1

SHE WAS DEAD when I got there.

"I'm sorry," the nurse said. "She told me to call you at this number. Then she just lay there with her eyes open. And then, just before you came, she closed her eyes and when I next glanced that way she'd gone. I'm sorry."

I looked at Aunt Jessie and, except that she seemed a kind of greenish yellow, she didn't appear that different from the way she did when she was alive. But a dead person is very dead, and I had never seen one before. I felt a little sick and swallowed. "It's all right," I said.

"Are you English?" the nurse said.

"No." And then because it seemed better to say

something than nothing, "I'm part Scottish, English and American."

"Oh. Well, the resident is coming back to talk to you. Would you like me to stay here with you, or maybe you'd like to wait out in the waiting room. Yes. That's better. Why don't you wait out there?"

"What's a resident?"

"He's the doctor who was in charge of the case when your aunt was brought in from Emergency. You know, I mean we have to find out who's the next relative. The next adult relative. She had no identification and we only called you because she said your name and gave me your number."

We were walking out of the room as the nurse talked. And I knew right away that I had to get out of there before this resident or doctor showed up.

"Is there a men's room around here?" I asked her.

"Sure, Alan. Right down that hallway to the right."

I was about to go when a terrible thought hit me. The nurse had Aunt Jessie's telephone number when she called me. If she still had it that meant she knew where to find me again.

"By the way," I said. "I haven't lived with Aunt Jessie too long and don't know her telephone number —know it off by heart, I mean. And now I have to call my uncle. Do you have the number with you?"

She put her hand in her pocket. "I think—yes, here it is. The number is—"

I snatched the paper out of her hand. No need to

give her time to learn it herself. "That's all right, Miss. I'd better take this—in case I forget."

She gave me a funny look then. I said quickly, "With my aunt dying and everything, I'm upset, and I can't be sure I'd remember it."

She smiled. She really wasn't so bad. "Sure, I understand. I suppose I was just surprised that she didn't ask me to call her husband."

"Husband?" I inquired stupidly, before I could realize what I was saying.

"Yes. Your uncle. Isn't that the person you said you were going to call? That's curious. I would have thought she'd have asked me to call him instead of you."

I could see that I'd made a serious mistake and had to do something about it before she started getting suspicious.

"Oh, I *see* what you mean. You thought I meant her *husband* when I said my uncle, didn't you?"

I was standing on one foot and then on the other, which is what I do when I get nervous, because I was trying frantically to think how I could have an uncle that wasn't her husband. "I see," I said again. And then I actually did see. "You thought I meant *her* husband. The uncle visiting us is the husband of her sister."

"Oh."

I shifted my feet again. "He was just passing through, my uncle I mean, and is visiting us for a little. He wasn't home when you called, but he's probably back now. So I have to call him and tell him about Aunt Jessie."

She was still looking at me in a funny way, so I swallowed and then stared at her. I stared at her wide-eyed, then blinked rapidly several times. I could tell by her change of expression that she thought I was about to burst into tears. She stopped looking suspicious and started looking sympathetic.

"Are you sure you wouldn't like me to call him?"

"Yes," I said. "I think it's better if I call him. You see," I went on, seeing she didn't really believe me, "my uncle is . . . is a little afraid of women. Women he doesn't know," I added hastily, thinking she could easily ask then why he was coming to visit Aunt Jessie.

The nurse just stood there looking at me. I pulled out a handkerchief and blew my nose. "I guess I'll go to the men's room first," I said, knowing I sounded choked up.

"Yes, of course. The resident will be here by the time you've done that and called your uncle."

That was exactly what I was afraid of. So I put my handkerchief to my face again, in case she expected me to say something, and made for the men's room.

I was in luck, it was empty, so I stayed long enough to tear up the paper with my aunt's telephone number on it and throw the pieces down the toilet and flush it.

When I came out of the men's room I saw the nurse and a man in a white coat and some others going towards the room where my aunt was. I knew the moment for me to get out had come. The nurse might send one of those men to look for me any minute. The elevators were right down the hall, but straight in front was a door marked "Stairs," and I decided that it was safer for me to escape that way.

Glad I had worn my sneakers, I made myself walk, not run, to the door, then quickly through. I met a couple of people in white coats on the stairs, and one nurse. But they didn't pay any attention to me, so when I got onto the ground floor, I just walked down the long hall, through the big lobby and out the door.

When I got outside a bus was coming along, so I took it and sat and thought about how things would be from now on and what I would have to do.

Maybe I'd better explain how I came to be riding uptown on a First Avenue bus in New York City, planning, now that Aunt Jessie was dead, how the Animal Kingdom and I could live alone in peace without being interfered with by a bunch of adults.

My parents, who were Scottish and English, emigrated over here, where they met and married and had me. When I was three they died in an accident and I got sent to live with my Aunt Margaret outside Chicago. But after a while she got ill, so I was sent to Scotland to live with my Uncle Ian. Then he went out to work in Japan, so I came back over here to live with a cousin in St. Louis. But she got married and her husband wasn't too keen on having a ready-made son of seven, so I was sent back to Scotland to live with Uncle Ian again, after he'd finished his job in Japan. I lived there for quite a while and went to school. Then Uncle Ian came to Canada, bringing me along, and I went to school there, and then he came down to Detroit, where he got a job in a car factory.

When you go to school in a lot of different places, one of the things you find out is that, no matter where you are, everybody thinks you talk funny. My accent, in the words of one of the teachers I wasn't crazy about, becomes "a focus of amusement." It's easier just to keep your mouth shut most of the time. Also, I started to stutter when I was about nine, which just made the focus more amusing than ever. It's less of a hassle to be called stupid because you don't talk than to have everybody holding their ribs together while some stand-up comic talks about l-l-leaving the d-d-d-door cl-cl-cl-closed. One of the things I like about animals is that they don't care how you talk.

It was while I was staying with Uncle Ian the second time that I discovered animals. We lived in a top floor flat in Glasgow and my room was a sort of half attic right under the roof which I liked a lot. One day a man came with a big tube-looking thing and traps and said that we had mice and that he had come to get rid of them. I had heard noises after I'd gone to bed—kind of a scuttling in the walls and one or two squeaks—and I'd thought they might be mice. But I liked the noises they made; they kept me company at night. So after the man had gone I sprang all the traps.

There wasn't much I could do about the poison the man sprayed down, but I stuffed all the mouse holes so they couldn't come out, and kept the windows open for a few days, and after that it was safe. Well, that led to bringing home bits of cheese and saving stuff from my dinner, so soon I had a regular colony. There was Mr. and Mrs. Mouse and Washington and Jefferson and Robert and Bruce and Lady Nelson. Actually, I didn't know which was what, if you follow me, and it turned out to be Washington who had the babies. It didn't really matter. But one day when I got home from school that man had come again and sprayed some awful stuff down the holes. All the colony had come out because they'd become tame, and they were now dead, and it was all my fault. I wouldn't speak to anyone for days after that. Every time I started to explain about the colony to Uncle Ian or anybody else, I'd stutter so much that I couldn't.

Uncle Ian wasn't so bad. He tried to understand and bought me a hamster that I named Reverend, after the minister who was Uncle Ian's chief friend. I took Reverend with me to Canada, when we moved there. But we weren't in Canada for very long before we went down to Detroit, where I got Bruce—short for Robert the Bruce—who was mostly Labrador, and Lana, the cat, named after some actress that Uncle Ian would talk about after he'd had a beer or two. Then Uncle Ian got killed in an assembly line accident, and I was sent to an orphanage till Aunt Jessie, who was really my great-aunt, finally came and got me. But by that time Bruce and Lana and Reverend were dead. They were killed because people from the child welfare society or what-

ever it's called turned up to take me to the orphanage.
I kept telling them I was going to live with Aunt Jessie
and I would take Bruce and Lana and Reverend with
me, but they took them anyway to the pound and killed
them. They—the child welfare people—said they
didn't have any facilities for taking care of pets. So that
was when I swore my oath: It's pretty silly and childish,
but I pricked my finger with a paper clip and swore in
blood on the family Bible, which I'd inherited, that I'd
never again tell any adults anything. All they ever do
is take charge of your life and ruin it.

Which was why I'd told all those lies at the hospital.
Now I had Winchester, Muff, Alexis, Wallace and Mr.
and Mrs. Gerbil to worry about, especially since Mrs.
Gerbil was expecting. And I wasn't about to play the
grownup's game of being Straight Arrow Honest Dan,
and have some truck come and take away the Animal
Kingdom, all the time explaining that the local orphanage or welfare society didn't have room for pets.

This is one reason why dealing with grownups is so
difficult. Mr. Ferguson, the minister of Uncle Ian's
church, was against lying. "Lies are practically the
worst sin there is," he'd said once. "Never, never, never
lie. Tell the truth and shame the devil."

In a queer way I knew he was right: lies were bad.
But then where was Mr. Ferguson when they came
with a truck and put Bruce, Lana and Reverend inside
and took them away and gassed them? Off telling somebody how to save his soul by not lying, probably.
Grownups are always telling you to tell the truth, be

16

candid, don't be afraid. But then, when you do tell the truth, the way I did in Detroit when I told the welfare society that I hadn't made any arrangements for Bruce and Lana and Reverend to be adopted, they do something horrible so that you know the whole thing is a plot to get power over you and take away your animals and have them destroyed. So you just have to be very careful to remember at all times that their rules are for them, and are made so that things work out their way. The moment the nurse called me and told me Aunt Jessie had had that heart attack and to come immediately, I stood in the middle of her living room and reminded myself about adults and their rules and how none of them is to be trusted, especially when it comes to animals. Then I said a prayer to St. Francis because he is the patron saint of animals, and he's the only one with power in heaven that I ever heard of who cares what happens to animals. Then I took the crosstown bus over to Second Avenue, and took the Second Avenue bus all the way downtown to the hospital. And when I got there Aunt Jessie had just died.

The nurse in charge told me that my aunt had no identification on her at all—no handbag, nothing. And since she was unconscious, they had no way of letting anyone know about her having had the attack. Then she came to, must have remembered me, told the nurse who was with her my name, Alan, and the telephone number, and the nurse said she wrote it down immediately on her pad so she wouldn't forget it. Then Aunt Jessie passed out again and died while I was on the way to the hospital. So if what the nurse told me was true, except for the paper I flushed down the john in the men's room, they had no way of knowing who I was, or where I lived, and if St. Francis was minding the store as I'd asked him to, the nurse wouldn't remember the number. Just to make sure he was, I closed my eyes on the bus and said a short prayer, reminding St. Francis of his responsibilities: Winchester, Muff and the others, all of whom needed his concentrated attention for the immediate future.

So now you know why it's important for me to keep adults out of the Animal Kingdom. Every now and then when I'd seen an adult walking his own dog at night I'd think maybe some of them could be trusted. But when it comes to what Uncle Ian used to call The Authorities, you can never be sure. They—the adults—nearly always knuckle under to The Authorities.

I really thought Aunt Jessie would be one of the worst. She was kind of old, and had once lived in a huge house on Fifth Avenue where she'd been a sort of housekeeper. And she looked like the kind of person who thought that everything had a place and there was a place for everything. And she was. So when I started bringing home animals, I was braced for a fight. But, though she never acted like she actually liked them, she never said anything except, "He'll need a lot of feeding up," or, "With a coat like that you'll have to be doing a lot of brushing," or, "Be sure and see that he gets plenty of meat." Other than that she never said much of anything, and neither did I. We weren't exactly close. Sometimes I thought that the reason she put up with the animals was that she knew I needed something she couldn't give me. Anyway, whatever it was, it was okay by me.

And now she'd had a heart attack and died, and if I knew anything at all about Authorities, they'd come and take my dog, and my cat, and my white rat and hamster and gerbils away and that'd be the end of them. That was why it was so important not to leave any address behind or anything that could tell them where Aunt Jessie and I had lived. I guessed that they'd have to search about because of things like getting Aunt Jessie buried. But, to quote one of the few things she'd say every now and then, first things first, and the Animal Kingdom staying alive came first.

So, as I rode uptown on the First Avenue bus, got off at 86th Street and got onto another bus going crosstown to the west side, I thought about how I could manage.

And the more I thought, the more I realized that the luckiest thing of all was that Aunt Jessie was what Mrs. Moscovich down the street called "a genuine eccentric."

Actually, Mrs. Moscovich called her an eccentric because she always tied up her garbage in newspaper and string so that it was a neat package with a bow, and she'd stand on the curb holding it in her arms until the garbage men came to collect it from her personally. The garbage men thought she was something like a saint, and when I saw the stuff streaming out of garbage cans and all over the street up and down from the house where we lived, I could see why they said so. But another way she was eccentric was her attitude towards banks. She didn't like them.

"Never have anything to do with banks, Alan Mac-Gowan," she said to me on the bus from Detroit, right after she'd come to collect me from the orphanage. "They just take your money and that's the last you hear of it. I know what I'm saying. Mr. Sedgewick-Carter, he was a banker, and look what he did: went to jail for taking the money from poor people who had trusted him."

Aunt Jessie had worked for the Sedgewick-Carters during something called The Depression, and among the poor people from whom he had taken money was Aunt Jessie, who had put ten years' savings in his bank. Since then she'd kept her money in what she called her strong box. After I'd been living with her a few months she told me about it, but no one else knew of it. And she kept it in her clothes closet under a stack of newspapers and hat boxes.

Of course, I had never actually seen inside her strong box, but whenever we needed money, she'd disappear into her closet and there'd be a great noise of newspaper rattling and then she'd emerge with the money for the rent or the telephone or Con Edison bill or groceries. Aunt Jessie paid cash for everything—sometimes sending me with it—or she sent me to the post office to buy a money order.

Thinking about this and other things as I got off the

bus and walked three blocks to the apartment, I began to see how things could work out.

I realize this makes me sound pretty cold-blooded, as though I didn't care at all that poor old Aunt Jessie had had a heart attack in the street and then died in the hospital. But the truth was, well, I did and I didn't. I didn't because during the year I'd lived with her we hardly ever talked. Mostly she walked around the streets looking at fruit and vegetables or watched television or read the Bible. She put up with the animals, as I said, but didn't have too much to do with them herself. I think she felt that, besides making up to me for not having friends because of my moving around a lot and my stammer, they were also a kind of bribe for not hanging out with the street kids whom she hated.

In fact, she was afraid of the street kids. Some kids had broken into an old woman's apartment across the street and trashed it because the old woman had called the cops on them for making too much noise under her window. Once, when some of the rowdier ones yelled after Aunt Jessie when she and I were coming home from church, and yelled after me, too, she went the color of her white wool scarf and walked straight ahead, her eyes not moving. I knew I could have joined with them, but I didn't. For one thing, it would have been scummy, and for another, it wouldn't have done any good, anyway. The moment I opened my mouth I would have given them all the material they needed for a year of comic turns. Anyway, the next day, Aunt Jessie brought home a gold-beige hamster in a cardboard carton and said, as she handed him to me, "You're not to let him in my room. You understand! I can't stand the vermin. And vermin he is, no matter what they call him!"

Aunt Jessie didn't say the hamster was for walking beside her through the street gang, but I was pretty sure it was. Because, along with being so white, I could see she was shaking, which was maybe why I took her arm. Or maybe it was because I was feeling funny, too. Right behind me, as I walked beside her, I heard a click, and I kept thinking that that was the way a switchblade would sound. When we got home she stood in the middle of her sitting room and said, "You understand, Alan, I'm not shaking because I'm afraid of yon hyenas, but because I'm *enraged.*" And her round blue eyes glared at me from behind her spectacles.

"Yes, Aunt Jessie," I said. Well, she probably *was* enraged—so was I. But I'd bet another new hamster that she was scared, too. Those kids—some of them—had ripped off the newsstand at the corner down the avenue and all but killed the old man. "Thanks for the hamster," I said. "I'll keep him in my room with the rest of the Kingdom."

I named the hamster Wallace, after the Scottish hero, and with some of the money I'd saved from baby-sitting, taking down the garbage for some of the tenants in our building and doing odd jobs around the neighborhood, I bought him a big cage with a wheel and a ladder and other deluxe hamster items, and I put it on the shelf next to Alexis's cage. Alexis is a white rat and, as a matter of fact, except when I'm out, he's never in his cage. Alexis likes either to be on the floor exploring, or in my pocket or on my shoulder. His middle name is F for friendly, which is nice for me, but worries me when it comes to other people he shouldn't be so friendly with. But I've always been pretty careful to see that no one knew about what Aunt Jessie called Alan's Animal Kingdom except, of course, for Aunt Jessie and me.

Anyway, it was because of worrying over what might happen to the animals that I couldn't spend too much time feeling bad about Aunt Jessie on my way home from the hospital. Because of Uncle Ian, Bruce, and Lana and Reverend I knew what people did when children were left with animals. That was when I discovered that children and animals didn't have any rights. I told this to Aunt Jessie when we were on the bus going to New York.

"Old people don't either, Alan," she said.

Which sounded to me pretty silly, but maybe was true.

Aunt Jessie lived on the top floor of what was called a renovated tenement house. The apartment was long, like a train, with a long narrow hallway, and with the rooms opening off one side, and the kitchen and bath at the front. The kitchen came first, then the bathroom, then Aunt Jessie's bedroom, her sitting room next to that, and the animals and I lived in the room at the other end.

When I got to our apartment, which is on the top

floor, Winchester, who looks like an oversized beagle with bassett ears, and Muff, the cat, met me at the door. I let Winchester express his pleasure at seeing me safe and sound after an absence of at least two hours, while Muff wound in and out of my legs. Muff is white with one blue and one green eye. After a few seconds there was a scratching of feet and Alexis came running along. Since he and Muff were brought up together they think they're out of the same litter. And every now and then I see Muff, who is really still a kitten, patiently licking Alexis all over. Alexis looks as though he sort of endures it but isn't sure what she's trying to do. I bent down now and picked him up and put him on my shoulder, where he nuzzled my neck. Then I went into the room at the back and checked out the gerbils and Wallace. Mrs. Gerbil was in front of the cage scratching frantically, which made me think she was probably trying to build a nest. I went to Wallace's cage, stroked him for a while, then put him inside my collar for a minute or two.

I checked on everybody's food and water, put Wallace in his cage and Alexis on the floor and then sat down and wrote a note from Aunt Jessie to Mr. Laurence, who is the headmaster of St. Alban's School—the school I go to—and rector of St. Alban's Church, Aunt Jessie's church. I had thought this out on the way home from the hospital and decided that the best reason for me to have been out of school that morning was to have gone to the doctor. I looked at the clock. It was around noon.

Aunt Jessie, who always waked up around four in

the morning, used to go shopping as soon as some of the vegetable and fruit stalls around our area opened up, which was around seven. There were stalls on the avenue stretching twenty blocks both north and south and ones Aunt Jessie liked even better way downtown on both the west and the east side. So lots of times she'd take the bus down and across and go around all the stalls, feeling and pinching and buying a little here and there. Then she'd bring home what she'd bought and can it or freeze it, which, she said, saved money, because then we wouldn't have to buy expensive stuff in the winter or get cans or frozen food. Personally, I think she did it just because she liked to go and look at the fruit and vegetables brought in fresh by truck every day to the city. It was while she was lugging a heavy bag of oranges from the lower east side that she'd had her attack. That must have been a little after seven, because the call from the hospital came just before I was going to leave for school. Well, at school they'd be having lunch from twelve to one, and then classes would start again at one thirty. I decided to have a sandwich and then go to school in the afternoon.

What I would really have liked to do would be to take Winchester to the park for the afternoon. But Mr. Laurence, who pokes his nose into everything, would probably call. If kids were out half a day or something, he'd grunt, but would take it. But if they were out a whole day he'd start asking questions like, "Why did it take the whole day?" Or, "What were you being examined for besides leprosy, the bubonic plague and the breakdown of the entire cardiovascular system?" Ha ha. At least, he wouldn't say anything so corny and obvious as ha ha. But he'd be wearing what Aunt Jessie always called his ironic look.

In other words, he didn't believe you, no matter what the note said, and did really nasty things like calling the parents or guardians or whomever and getting it straight from the horse's mouth, as he said, and then added, not that he trusted the horse, either.

I was just reading over the note saying that I went to the doctor for earache, when the phone rang. For a while I thought some terrible ESP was working and that Mr. Laurence had picked up my vibrations and was calling.

I stared at the phone as it rang the second, third and fourth times. Then I picked it up. "Hello."

"Is this the residence of—er—Miss Jessie MacAndrews?"

It sounded as though someone was reading off a name and my heart gave a thunk. I was sure it was the hospital.

"Who is this?" I asked, because I couldn't think of anything else to say.

I was right. It was the hospital. I pinched my nostrils together with one hand and put on a Spanish accent, or at least what I hope sounded like a Spanish accent.

"You gotta the wrong numero."

"What?"

"Wrong number," I yelled, forgetting the accent, and hung up.

I stood there and after a minute I was shaking all over. That crummy nurse must have remembered the number. For a moment I had what I thought was a good idea: I'd rip out the telephone cable the way I'd seen them do in the movies and on TV. But before I could do more than give the wire a yank, I knew it would be the dumbest thing I could do. Aunt Jessie said she only had the phone in case she got sick or something. But I knew that Mr. Laurence might call if he was feeling suspicious, which is what he seems to feel most of the time, and if he got some funny sound on the line, especially knowing Aunt Jessie was old and had a weak heart, he'd call the telephone company—or the police —and they'd be over practically in five minutes and I'd be explaining everything all the way to the juvenile center. And the animals—but I wasn't going to think about that.

I really didn't like the idea that the nurse had remembered the number, so, with the Kingdom in mind, I said a prayer to St. Francis that the hospital would decide that they'd got hold of the wrong number and everyone would leave us alone.

After lunch I left for school, trying to keep Winchester from barking too loud so that Mrs. Schuster, downstairs, wouldn't complain for the umpteenth time that he was destroying her afternoon meditation. Mrs. Schuster says she is practicing to be a yoga. Or maybe yogi. Anyway, in some way I've never understood, Winchester interferes with her merging with the Infinite.

Aunt Jessie sent me to St. Alban's School, instead of the public school, because she said (and I quote, because she said it a lot) a body shouldn't grow up without a firm grounding in the Scripture.

She didn't ask me, she just said the day after I got to New York, "Alan, tomorrow morning I will take you to St. Alban's School where I entered you before I left for Detroit. Mr. Laurence, the headmaster, who is also rector of the kirk (which is Scottish for church), is taking you as a special favor to me, so you must work hard and be a good boy." Which is the kind of thing adults always tag onto the end of practically everything they say. Except, I've got to give him credit, Mr. Laurence. Not that he's Mr. Friendly, or that I'd trust him with information about the Animal Kingdom, but he had a different way of giving the jab. "Try and do the minimum damage, Alan," is more in his style.

Because of my speech problem I don't talk much around school. This way I can keep down the usual static about my stammer. In a way it would be easier if it was there all the time—my stammer, I mean. I've known kids with a stammer who tripped practically on every word, and while they run into the usual unpleasantness, once people got used to it, they were inclined to forget about it. Mine hits only when I get upset or nervous, so it's hilarious news every time.

Anyway, because of it, I don't talk much, but I listen a lot, and one of my favorite topics around the classroom and yard is how a really cool female—good-looking and years younger than The Sludge (which is what everybody calls Mr. Laurence)—could have ever stumbled into marriage with him.

There are various theories: one is that he blackmailed her; that she made the mistake of confessing to him (a clergyman) that she had had an illegitimate child and he held it over her to get her to marry him. The trouble with that was that there was no child, illegitimate or otherwise, so the theory suffered from what the detective flicks call lack of hard evidence.

Betsy Howard, who's in my class and is a feminist, said that made Mrs. Laurence into nothing more than a sex object and she was worth a lot more than that, which may be true. But whenever I think about the way she crinkles up her eyes at the corners when she laughs, I like it a lot, so I try and think of things to make her laugh. She teaches English and composition at the school, and we get along, because those are my best subjects.

The trouble is, since I want to be a vet, my best subject ought to be science, which is taught by Mr. Bryant, when he isn't coaching in gym and sports. Mr. Laurence teaches science to the older kids. I'm in Mr. Bryant's class, which is better than being in Mr. Laurence's simply because he's more human, but it still isn't good. For one thing, Mr. Bryant doesn't appreciate my attitude towards sports, which is that they are dumb activities for dumb people, and the other is that, even though I know it's part of the necessary education to be a vet, I don't like dissecting things. The whole state of affairs between us has been going downhill since the day he told me to stop pussyfooting around and get on with the frog I was supposed to be dissecting. I said I wasn't training to be a butcher. He told me to stand up and state what profession I wanted to enter (in a weak moment I'd told him about wanting to be a veterinarian). I knew that was so he could then enlighten the class about the knowledge of anatomy and science necessary to be a vet. So I just kept my seat and told him okay I'd take the poor, lousy dead frog apart. But the words stuck. That is, I started to stutter on the first consonant. There were a few giggles. Bryant grinned. Everybody laughed. Bryant said, okay, that was enough. But I sat there wishing he were dead and the others dying horribly. I picked up the dissecting knife —and threw up. The whole episode was a triumph all around.

Even so, and repulsive as he was, I knew he wouldn't be as bad as The Reverend Sludge. He taught Scripture to the whole school, that is, to all the classes, not just the younger ones. And although it is against my principles to admit that I liked it, first of all because Mr. Laurence taught it, and second of all because it's such a pie-in-the-sky thing to like, the truth is, there are a lot of good stories in the Bible. Not that you'd know it from Mr. Laurence. Most of the time he was like something out of a bad joke: stiff, narrow, you-do-it-my-way-or-else. And if he was that way about Scripture, he'd be ten times more that way with science. So I stuck with the lesser of two teaching evils, Mr. Bryant. But Mr. Laurence was headmaster and I still had to get my absences okayed by him.

The school occupies three tenement buildings that are on the other side of the parish hall. Most of the insides of the buildings were taken out, or at least walls were knocked down, and the bigger rooms that were left were turned into classrooms and connecting doors were made so that you don't have to run outside every time you want to go from one old building to another. Next to the three buildings is what had once been a parking space, but which some well-wisher had bought and given to the school. This is the recreation ground where we play ball and at the back of that is a large shed that holds the gym. It's not exactly the playing fields of Eton, but it's okay, and although I wouldn't want anyone to know it, I found it easier to cope with that than a school like the one I'd been to in Detroit where the most successful teaching program—how to be a terrorist—went on in the halls and classrooms most of the time. If you're skinny and small and have a funny accent and stammer, and don't hang around with people, then it's a good idea to have some karate lessons to compensate. Uncle Ian taught me a few dirty tricks, but they're only really useful on a one-to-one basis. If a bunch decides to close in, then the best defense is an ability to run. Luckily, I'm very good at that and back in Scotland won a couple of prizes for the hundred-yard sprint.

I went now into the first house, where Mr. Laurence's office is. I knocked at his door, hoping he wasn't in, so I could leave the note on his desk. Unfortunately, he was. "Come in," he yelled.

I went in, mumbled good afternoon and put the note on his desk. Then I made for the door.

"Not so fast, Alan," he said.

I turned slowly.

He slit open the envelope. "Stick around."

"I'm due for gym," I said, back to the door. Nothing good, I felt, could come out of my standing there while he read the note.

"I'll give you permission to be late for gym," he said, and waved a hand. "Sit down."

I didn't sit. I stood with my back to him, looking at pictures and notices on a big bulletin board.

"I see your aunt's arthritis is still bothering her," he said.

I jumped. "Arth—th—th-thritis?" I said. There it went again. I started to make myself breathe slowly.

He was sitting at his desk holding the note. I once heard someone say Mr. Laurence's eyes were hazel, whatever color that is. I'd say they were a greenish brown, and right now they reminded me of two gun barrels.

"Yes," he said, "Arthritis. The reason you have to write all these notes for her. Remember?"

Too late, as usual, I remembered. It was true Aunt Jessie did have arthritis and she had asked me to write a couple of notes for her. But I had also given that as an excuse for a couple of notes she didn't know she'd written. Like the day I went to the cat show and wrote a note from Aunt Jessie saying I was at the dentist, and another time when I went to a pet store downtown that advertised budgies and wrote a note saying I was at the doctor.

"Is she seeing a physician about it?"

"Oh yes. She sees one all the time." I started standing on one foot and then on the other. Sometimes if I do that I don't stammer so much.

"The same one you saw for your ear?"

"No. That was a different one."

"All those different doctors run to a lot of money." Pause. I breathed very slowly. In. Out. And shifted my feet again.

"Nervous, Alan?"

I stopped changing feet. "Er n-no?"

"Then why are you hopping about like that?"

"I have to go to the bathroom," I said.

He waved a hand towards the door opening out of his office. "Be my guest."

The trouble was, I'd been, just before leaving the house, so it took me a while.

"You okay?" he asked, when I came out.

"Fine." I was pleased to see I had got that out without stuttering. I took another breath. "I'd better go to the gym now."

He looked at me a minute. "Okay. But you've never struck me before as one of the school's more ardent athletes."

"P-people ch-change." That was one of the other

teachers' favorite expressions. I suddenly realized I was moving my feet again, and he was looking at them.

"Not that much," he said, his eyes boring into my feet.

I guess that's why I find that lying is not really worth it, unless it's absolutely necessary, like now. To use one of Aunt Jessie's sayings, it takes it out of one.

"Okay," he said suddenly. "Go on to the gym. Tell Mr. Bryant that you've been with me."

And don't think I wasn't glad to get sprung from that. The only thing was, I now had to go to gym, which I'd been hoping to get out of, but it would be just like The Sludge to check up on me.

2

THAT EVENING, on the way home from school, I bought three pieces of pizza and two chocolate ice-cream sodas and took them home for dinner. Leaving the sodas in the freezer, I took Winchester out for a walk in Riverside Park and we had a good time running for an hour or so. I take a leash along because the law says that dogs are not supposed to be off leash, and there are not only cops about, but there are dog-hating snoops whose whole mission in life seems to be to have dogs sent to the pound. Winchester likes to sprint and so do I, so we had a good time competing, except that he won every time. But I didn't mind.

It was about time to go home when I saw some of the local gang come into the other end of this section of the park. The gang's always been around, at least since I've lived here, but recently, in the last couple of weeks, a new leader, Stud Clancy, had taken over. Under him the gang had suddenly become meaner and more aggressive, pushing north into this part of the park and even occasionally into our street, bothering kids and animals and old people.

"Hey, there's that dog," one of them yelled, and they started off after Winchester, who had been scratching around a small tree.

It's lucky I have a really piercing whistle, which is helped by the fact that one of my front teeth has a corner chipped off, so I can whistle through it. I whistled now for Winchester and he came loping towards me. Then I whistled twice, which means *run* and he started to gallop flat out towards me. But even so, some of the gang, who were between Winchester and me, were running to cut him off.

I was scared to the point of feeling sick, but ran towards Winchester and the kids, when I guess St. Francis must have been really paying attention, because David Haines, one of the big kids from my school, suddenly appeared like he'd come up out of the ground, there, not far from Winchester. Now David, who is black, doesn't talk much more than I do. But nobody fools around with him. For one thing, he's seventeen and nearly six feet. For another, he's on the basketball team and an honor student.

"David," I yelled. "That's my dog."

David looked around, and then ran easily in a couple of long strides, got hold of Winchester by the collar and shoved him behind him.

The three kids in front stopped. "That's our dog," they said. But you could tell they didn't think he'd believe them.

"Yeah?" David said. "You wanna come with me and tell that to the cops at the precinct?"

They said a few words but slid away. David watched them go, then released Winchester, who jumped up, licked him and ran towards me. That's the trouble with Winchester, dumb dog that he is. He would have licked the three kids and been Mr. Friendly, that is, until they tried to drag him away. He's pretty clear about whose dog he is.

"Thanks," I said.

"S'okay." David, who was in jeans, a sweat shirt and sneaks, had been jogging. "Nice dog. Where'd you get him?"

"From the street. Somebody tied him up to the railing of the house opposite. And there he was in the rain, crying, for a couple of hours. I went across and rang all the bells in case he belonged to somebody who was visiting one of the tenants. But the guy in the basement said some man had come there in the early morning, tied him up, then gotten in his car and driven away. He was only a puppy."

David was looking at him. "He's still only a puppy, for all his size."

"Yeah. I took him to the vet, who said he was about four months. That was six months ago."

David straightened. "It'd be smarter not to run him in the park when those kids are around. Try some other time."

"The trouble is, I'm in school."

"Well then, you might as well expect trouble. S'long." And David loped off towards the end of the block.

I put Winchester on the leash and took him the long way around the block and got him safely back home. Then I fed Winchester and Muff and ate the pieces of pizza and chocolate sodas, which were now like frozen soup. That still left a lot of the evening. But I cleaned out all the cages, and let Wallace, Alexis and the gerbils chase themselves around the floor while I changed the papers at the bottom and put water and food inside.

Then I sat around and watched television until it was time to go to bed. I didn't exactly miss Aunt Jessie, but it felt funny, being by myself. And I didn't go to sleep right away as I usually did. I kept thinking about her lying dead in the hospital and wondered what they did with dead people who were left there. My uncle Ian was cremated. My mother and father were taken back to Scotland to be buried.

And then, just as I was drifting off to sleep, I remembered that Aunt Jessie had said that she wanted to be buried back in Scotland. And I lay there, wide awake again. I supposed if I went to the hospital and told them Aunt Jessie wished to be buried in Scotland, somebody would do something and she would be, although I didn't know how.

But if I did that they would know where I lived, and I suddenly saw Winchester being dragged away into a truck and put into a gas chamber. And Muff and Alexis and the others. "I'm sorry, Aunt Jessie," I said aloud. Suddenly it felt funny saying that. As though there were really somebody in the room to hear me. I could feel Winchester lying against my legs and put my hand down. He licked it and slobbered over it gently. Then he started to scratch and I could feel the whole bed shaking. Muff, who was on the other side of my legs, must have felt the vibrations and waked up. Because I could feel her coming up towards my face. Then she curled herself around and around and settled in a ball on my pillow. I had drawn the blinds on all the windows, in case anybody should see in and wonder where Aunt Jessie was. But I decided I really didn't like the dark when it was so black I couldn't even see Muff's white fur. So I got up and drew up the blind. Enough light came in for me to see the shapes of the cages around the room, the chair and the desk, and even though my bed was in a corner, I could see a small white blob on my pillow that was Muff and a huge dark blob that was Winchester. Then I went back to bed.

After a while I remembered that Aunt Jessie was supposed to be in heaven and tried to imagine how she would look up there. But all I could see was Aunt Jessie in her MacAndrew tartan skirt and hat with the fake cherries on it and her steel spectacles, sitting in the pew in church. No matter what, I couldn't see her in a white robe or on a cloud or bathed in a bright light. Finally I heard myself say, "Good night, Aunt Jessie," and again I felt queer, because it was like she was in the room. Then I went to sleep.

"Alan, did you read the assignment?"

It was The Sludge, asking stupid questions, as usual. I had forgotten all about homework, what with Aunt Jessie and the hospital and everything. I should have known that he would call on me. I debated for a moment about saying yes and trying to bluff it through. Some kids were really good at that, but I never was.

"Well?" The Sludge asked, and then, as I tried to think of a way out, added, "Surely you can't have too many options? The answer must be yes or no."

I hated him. "No," I said.

"Why not?"

"I didn't get around to it," I muttered.

"What did you say?"

"I d-d-didn't g-g-get around t-t-t-t—" The worst thing is to stick on a word. I heard the snickers, first in the back and then on the sides.

The Sludge brought his ruler down on the desk. "Stop that. At once!"

I'll say this for him. You could hear a pin drop. But it didn't prevent me from wishing I were dead or somewhere else.

"Alan, see me after the class. Next."

Of course I knew and everybody else knew what had occurred. If this had happened to one of the other kids, The Sludge would have made him admit he hadn't cracked the Bible and then given him an extra amount of work for the next time as punishment. But he wouldn't make me attempt to talk now. And I suppose he was trying to be fair, but it was almost as bad as trying to talk. Just as I was leaving, when the class was over, following The Sludge to his office, I heard Betsy say, in a stage whisper, "Teacher's pets always get a private conference, don't they?"

I ignored it. What else could I do? I followed The Sludge into his office.

"Well, Alan," he said, walking over to and around his desk.

I didn't say anything.

The Sludge stood there behind his desk, turning over letters and papers, not looking at me. Then he said, "Have you ever had anyone to help you with your stammer?"

I don't like talking about my problem, even though I know that everybody (obviously) knows about it. I took a breath and let it out slowly and shifted my feet a little. "No," I said.

"I know somebody—a doctor—who's had some success in helping people."

"Doctors cost money," I said. It was something

Aunt Jessie used to say and it was the only thing I could think of.

He looked at me then, as though the worst was over. "I think that could be worked out."

Never, never allow yourself to be under obligation to anyone, Uncle Ian had always said. *Sooner or later, somehow, you'll have to pay. And it will be in a way you won't like.*

"I'd rather not."

"Why not? The Sludge was a big man with wide shoulders, and his round white collar and black front made him look bigger than ever. He was standing with his jacket pushed back behind his hands, which were on his hips. "Don't you want to be . . . free of . . . of this . . . impediment?"

I could tell he was trying to pick his words carefully, but it made me madder than ever.

"It's okay. I don't mind."

The silence was like a rubber band that was stretching further and further.

"Okay," he said finally. "It's your problem. The trouble is, it's also mine. If I put pressure on you in class then you start to stammer. The others laugh—and no matter what you say I know you don't like that. Who would? If I reprimand them then you become teacher's pet—Yes," he went on as I looked quickly at him, "I heard that. I'm pretty sure I was supposed to. I'd like to protect you, but for your own good I can't beyond a certain point. Which leaves us back where we started. Think it over. All right. For your punishment you're to do both yesterday's and today's assignment and I'll call on you in class tomorrow."

I moved my feet again. It helped me not to stammer. "Okay," I said. I could feel him staring at my back as I left the room.

That afternoon as I was coming out of basketball practice I ran into The Sludge's wife, that is, Mrs. Sludge, who is Mrs. Laurence.

"Hello, Alan," she said.

"Hello, Mrs. Laurence." I watched her eyes. Sure enough, they crinkled up at the corners and I saw that she was smiling. She really is neat-looking: medium tall, with a figure that goes in and out a lot, like it would be soft if you touched it. Betsy says that her figure is kind of old-fashioned, and that the right look for today is unisex. I know that's the word because somebody asked her to spell it. She said it was like unicorn, only sex instead of corn. But then Betsy's skinny and bossy.

I liked being there in the school yard with Mrs. Laurence, but since I couldn't think of anything to say, I was about to pass her when she said, "Would you give a message to your Aunt Jessie, Alan?"

It was as though she had hit me, and it was a shock, like Winchester suddenly biting me. I could feel my throat beginning to close up and freeze, which had never happened to me before with Mrs. Laurence. I must have showed the way I felt or jumped or something because she said suddenly, "Are you all right, Alan?"

I moved my feet, took a breath and let it out slowly.

"Sure," I said. I would have liked to say something else, but I was afraid to. The way my throat felt I'd start hitting some word or letter and not be able to come off.

"It's only," Mrs. Laurence went on, "that I tried to call her today to remind her of the meeting tomorrow in the parish hall. She must have been out. I might not get another chance to call. Would you remind her for me?"

Why hadn't I thought of that? Aunt Jessie was up to her elbows in church goings-on. She belonged to the Altar Guild and the Bible Fellowship and she sometimes taught Sunday School. I stood there, unable to think. All I could feel was panic. Then I heard myself saying, without knowing where it came from, "Well, Aunt Jessie's sister just came to town and got sick. She's way over on the east side. Aunt Jessie has to nurse her. She's going to be there practically all the t-t-t-time." I almost managed to get through it without sticking.

Mrs. Laurence's eyes weren't crinkling anymore and she wasn't smiling. "I'm sorry to hear that. I wonder if there's something I can do to help."

The panic closed in again. "No. Aunt Jessie's sister doesn't want anybody else. That's the whole trouble. Only Aunt Jessie."

"I see. That makes it hard for your aunt. You know I didn't know she had any sisters. I thought I heard her say once that she was the only girl in her family. But I guess I'm wrong."

"She isn't really her sister. They were brought up

together. That's why I call her Aunt . . . Aunt Mary. They're very close."

"You seem very nervous, Alan. Is there something wrong?"

When people say that I usually say I have to go to the bathroom. But I didn't like to say it to Mrs. Laurence. Instead I said, "Am I? I g-g-guess I'm hungry."

"Is your aunt going to be there to fix dinner for the two of you?"

"Oh sure. She's always there for dinner."

"Good. If I get a chance I'll call her tonight. There's something I want to ask her."

I felt so strung out after that conversation that I stopped on the way home and had a soda. When I finished that I ordered a second one, but in the middle of it I started to feel sick, so I left the rest and went on home.

Winchester all but knocked the door down he was so glad to see me and so eager to go for our walk. I was thinking about what to do, whether to take him a block up before I got to the park or just to run him up and down the avenue, when I happened to look out the front window. There was David Haines coming up out of the basement apartment across the street in his sweat shirt, the same one he had on the day before. I pushed up the window. "Hey, David," I yelled.

He looked around.

"Up here."

Finally he saw me. "Yeah?"

"I'm just coming down. I'll go with you. I want to take Winchester out."

"That's no good. You can't keep up with me."

"Yes I can. And so can Winchester. Stay there." I slammed down the window in case he was going to say no, snatched up Winchester's leash, and the two of us hurled ourselves downstairs. David was almost at the park by the time we got outside, so Winchester and I tore after him. He must have heard us, because just as he was going through the railings into the park he stopped and turned, waiting for us.

"Look," he said when we caught up, "I have to cover a lot of ground before six, when I have to be home for dinner. Why don't you exercise your dog early in the morning before school? The park's practically empty then except for a few joggers and bird watchers. The gang doesn't show up till later in the day."

"Well, I will from now on, but he hasn't had his run today. Besides, I can keep up with you. I won the hundred-yard dash at my last school."

David ran his eye up and down me, and I had a feeling he thought I was making it up.

"Lots of track stars are skinny," I said.

"I can't stop you," he said. "But I'm not going to wait if you can't keep up." And he turned and started to lope off towards the north end of the park.

I guess it was that day I learned the difference between a sprint and an hour's steady jogging. David didn't look as though he were putting out effort at all. He hardly sweated. But after about ten minutes I would have liked to stop and walk. After about twenty minutes I had to stop pretending he wasn't gaining on me. By that time he was almost out of sight, way ahead of me up the park. And Winchester was with him. After about half an hour I was tired and feeling a little light in the head. Then I stumbled. So I sat down on a bench. As soon as I could get my breath I whistled as loudly as I could.

As I did I felt the bench move. I looked around and saw what I hadn't noticed before: at the other end sat an old man. In front of him on the ground sat a small mutt that looked like a cross between a Chihuahua and a Boston terrier. It was gray around the muzzle so I could see it was old, too.

The old man turned then and I could see he was Chinese or an Oriental of some kind. But when he spoke he sounded like anybody else in New York. "That's some whistle. You made me jump. And you scared Ming here."

"I was just whistling for my dog."

The old man looked around. "I don't see any dog."

That was the trouble: neither did I. "He's way up ahead with a friend." But the truth was, even though I liked David, I was worried whenever Winchester was out of sight. Only I had a stitch in my side that was nearly bending me double. I leaned over, holding my side. "How old's Ming?"

"About fourteen, as far as I can make out. He came off the street, so I'm not sure how old he was when I found him. About a year. That was thirteen years ago."

47

Just then, his long ears flowing back like the wings on a sweptwing jet, Winchester came in view. As soon as he located me he went into a flat-out gallop and flung himself at me, all but knocking over me, the bench and the old man.

"Down, Winchester. Get down. Down!" Eventually he calmed down and went over to inspect Ming, who paid no attention to him at all. But after a while I could see that Winchester was bothering the old dog so I got up to go.

"What did you say your dog's name is?" the old man asked.

"Winchester."

He started to smile. Then his face cracked into a laugh. "I named Ming, Ming because he was a mutt and the Mings were a ruling family of China for several centuries. I guess you named your dog for about the same reason."

"Sort of. I saw the name of a jar of marmalade that Aunt Jessie had and it seemed like a good name for Winchester when I got him. I mean it's better than Bowser or Boots or Bozo or one of those. It has character."

The old man was still smiling. "It does."

At that moment the thing I'd been dreading appeared: some of the street gang erupted into the southern end of the park, yelling and throwing a ball. I looked at them. "I think I'm going to go now," I said. "Come on, Win," and I put my hand on Winchester's collar.

48

"Is that the gang?" the old man said, and he sounded different, shaky and frightened. "Come here, Ming." He bent slowly, and I could see there was a cane on the other side of him. "Ming doesn't run too well," he said. "I thought David would be back by now."

I wanted to go in the worst way. The kids hadn't seen us yet, because there were some bushes in the way, but I could hear them getting nearer. But somehow, looking at Ming, I was still there. "I'll carry Ming, if you want, but I think we ought to go." Only I kept thinking, I wonder if he can walk fast enough. And then help came from two places. A whole bunch of people climbed over the railing from the drive, and David, still jogging, appeared at the far north end of the path.

At that moment the first two of the kids came around the bushes. "There's the old man," Stud Clancy, who was in front, said. He was about my age, but tall and thick, with long blonde hair. Right behind him came Lee Jennings, who's black, as tall as Stud, but thin and good-looking, with high cheekbones and a thin, straight nose.

Winchester, the idiot dog, barked.

"Let's take the dog," Lee said. The funny part was I knew it was kind of a super joke with him. His eyes were shining, and he looked like he was almost laughing. Lee had once been a student at St. Alban's and dropped out or was kicked out because of something to do with drugs. He didn't want Winchester, he wanted to annoy me. Stud was different. He'd kick or abuse anything he could get his hands on.

49

I handed Ming to the old man and whistled loudly through my broken tooth to bring back Winchester, who was about to do his friendship bit with Lee.

Winchester turned, practically in midair, and ran back. Stud took a long knife out of his waistband. David, running up, gave a shout. The people who had come from the drive—they looked like students from the university—picked up speed. Stud and Lee turned and saw them and took off.

By this time the students had come up. There were about eight of them and all of them had on jeans and sweat or T-shirts and I realized they were joggers, too. I was about to open my mouth and say thanks when I nearly fell over. Hidden by three of the students standing in front was—I couldn't believe it—The Sludge, also in jeans and sweat shirt. "Hello, Alan," he said.

I was so stunned I didn't even stammer. "Hello, Mr. Laurence. I didn't know you jogged."

"Do I look too old or too sedentary?" he said.

"Too old," I blurted out, and saw him wince.

"Well," he said. "I don't know that that's any less debilitating to the ego than looking sedentary."

"What does sedentary mean?" I asked. And then, "Here, Winchester, down." Because that stupid hound had decided that The Sludge was his new friend and was leaping around him practically saying, Here I am. Notice me. Let's have a game. Throw me a ball. "Come on, Winchester. Stop bothering him—Mr. Laurence."

"He doesn't bother me. And after your comment

about my age he's doing worlds for my ego. Did you say his name was Winchester? Where'd you get that?"

"Off a marmalade jar." I wasn't too sure I was pleased at all this love and affection going on between The Sludge and Winchester.

"Sedentary," Mr. Laurence said, rubbing Winchester between his ears, "means sitting down. A sedentary job is a job you do sitting down. Like teaching some of the time. More like somebody sitting in an office at a desk. If somebody looks sedentary it means he looks like he never gets any exercise."

"Oh." I looked at The Sludge and was bound to admit that he didn't look as though he never exercised. In fact, although it was hard to think about him that way when he was in that black suit, he looked tough, like David.

David. I suddenly realized he had disappeared and so had the old man and Ming, and so, for that matter, had all the students that had jogged up with Mr. Laurence.

"Well," I said, beginning to shift my feet, "I'd better be getting home."

"I'll come along with you."

"It's several blocks down," I said hastily.

"I know. That's all right. Old as I am I might just manage to struggle down that far. But if I suddenly crumble at the knees you'll know it's my advanced age."

I couldn't help it. I started to laugh. I'd had a

teacher back in Scotland who used to talk a little like that, like he was serious, only you knew he wasn't.

"Mr. Ross used to talk that way," I said, turning with him and starting to walk south along the path that led out into the drive.

"Who is, or was, Mr. Ross?"

"A teacher I had back in Scotland. He used to say things without laughing, only you knew he was laughing inside."

"Not laughing at you," The Sludge said quickly.

He gave me a quick glance down and I could see he looked a little worried.

"No. I didn't think you were. That's not what I meant."

"Okay. Just as long as you're clear about that. How long did you go to school in Scotland?"

"About three years. Before that I went to school for a year in St. Louis. I had almost a year in Canada after Scotland and one year in Detroit."

"You have moved around. It must make lessons— where you are and what you've been studying—very baffling."

"I don't mind the studying so much. I mean, I like to read the same things anywhere. . . ."

My voice trailed off, because it was hard to explain what I did find hard. And suddenly the fact that he said what he did made me feel like it was a huge load.

"But the changes in people are confusing?"

The moment he said it I knew he'd hit it.

"Yeah. They're all different. You never know where you are. Something's okay in Scotland, but over here everybody laughs. But then they did there, too, when I did something or said something American."

"I know what you mean."

That's the kind of thing adults say all the time and they don't know what they're talking about. But I knew he did know. I could tell by his voice. "You do?"

He looked down at me. "Sure. My people were missionaries. I grew up in China, India and parts of Africa, in the meantime going to school off and on here."

"But you had your parents, didn't you?" It was queer, my saying that. I couldn't even remember my mother and father, who died when I was a baby.

"Yes, I did. You don't remember yours, do you, Alan?"

I shook my head. "Here, Winchester," I yelled. And whistled through the gap in my tooth. Winchester, who had been ambling towards the park as though he thought I wouldn't notice, gave his funny jump and started running back towards me. "Keep out of the park," I said to him.

"Do you think he understands?" The Sludge asked.

"Of course. He understands everything. So does Muff."

"Another dog?"

"No, Muff's a cat. All white with one blue eye and one green one. She was in a garbage can one night a few months ago, and some kids—some of the same guys who run with Stud Clancy—were about to throw a cherry bomb in there with her."

There was a pause. "And you got her out?"

"Yes." Saying that made me feel funny and uncomfortable.

One of the things that bothers me, when I think about it, is that I'm not brave. I'd rather run away than fight, which is why Uncle Ian taught me all those tricks. "Ye have to stand yer ground sometime, Alan-boy. Sooner or later ye must meet yer own particular dragon. Maybe yours is to stand and fight." He said it with a great rolling of Rs, because Uncle Ian was brought up in Glasgow, and his accent was so thick that sometimes even I couldn't understand him.

"I didn't think," I said now. "I just got mad, grabbed the cherry bomb and threw it back at them just before it went off. Then I got Muff out and ran."

"Good for you."

I didn't say anything.

We walked for a while down the drive.

"What's bothering you?" The Sludge said suddenly. "It seems to me that you did well with Muff, getting her out of the garbage can."

"Well. . . . I don't like fighting. . . . The kid who was throwing in the bomb wasn't any bigger than I am, but I ran."

I couldn't believe I was saying this. Maybe it had something to do with the fact that The Sludge had on a sweat shirt rather than his black suit. I reminded myself that he was the headmaster of the school and probably untrustworthy and had just given me a double assignment for his crummy Scripture class.

"I don't think there's much to be said for the boy who goes around with his fists on the ready wanting to fight everybody. He's trying to hide something just as much as the boy who runs away. But if you think you run away when you should stand, then maybe you should have a few boxing lessons to give you confidence. But for heaven's sake don't feel that you're a coward because you run away from somebody bigger and stronger than you. That's just intelligent."

We walked for a few blocks without saying anything. Then, "How's your Aunt Jessie?" The Sludge asked. I'd been feeling pretty good until that moment. But the moment he said that I started feeling nervous.

"F-fine," I said.

"My wife mentioned that she couldn't get in touch with her about some meeting or other."

"Yeah. I know. She—Mrs. Laurence—talked to me today."

"I hope everything's all right."

"No." I took a deep breath and launched into my story. "She just went to see an old friend who's very sick and she's having to take care of her."

Sometimes when I make up something it gets truer every time I say it and I suppose I was hoping this would happen with my story about Aunt Jessie's sick friend. But it didn't. I was sure The Sludge was going to say, "You're lying." Just like that. And then he'd force his way upstairs or call the police or have the house watched or put out a radio or television call for Aunt Jessie, and all the time I'd be down at the police station, and the animals wouldn't have anybody with them and after a while they'd either starve or the ASPCA would come and take them away.

". . . so I could come upstairs and wait for her, at least for a few minutes."

"What?" I said, suddenly realizing what The Sludge was saying.

"I said I wanted to ask her something about taking an extra Sunday School class for the next week or so, so if she's home I'll come up with you and ask her now. Or if she'll be home anytime soon I could go up and wait a few minutes. Why are you looking like that?"

By this time we had stopped walking. There are times when The Sludge seems eight feet tall. This was one of those times. He was looking down at me, frowning.

"She's asleep. She gets very tired nursing her friend."

"I see. Well, will you ask her to call me when she wakes up."

I moved that around in my head and it seemed all right. "Sure. I mean, she fixes dinner and then goes right out again. I have to go now." And I started to break away.

"Just a minute." His long arm was out and he had me by the shoulder. "Is there anything any of us can do?"

Why did they all have to be so helpful? What good would they be if the sheriff or whoever would turn up with a truck and take away the animals? Probably they'd all still be there asking if there was anything they could do while Winchester and Muff and Wallace and the Gerbils and Alexis were all being gassed. After all, when Uncle Ian died there were a lot of people who came around saying they'd like to do something. But Bruce and Lana and Reverend were still taken away, even though I asked several people—ones who'd said they'd wanted to help—if they'd take Bruce or Lana or Reverend just until Aunt Jessie came and I could get them to New York. But they all either already had dogs or cats or hamsters or didn't want them. Wait until you get settled, they all said, and then you can buy yourself a new puppy or a new kitten—just like they were things without character or personality. I felt like asking them why they bothered so much about their stupid children —after all they could always get new ones and wouldn't even have to pay for them.

I yanked my shoulder free. "I have to go now," I said. "I've got to be there so she can get dinner as soon as she wakes up and get out, because she has a lot to do. G'bye."

And I took off, irritated at myself for letting him soft talk me into forgetting to be careful. "Ye canna be too cautious," Uncle Ian used to say, only he pronounced too, tiu. Anyway, he was right.

When Winchester and I went into the apartment Muff was sitting on one side of the hall and Alexis on the other. The moment we came in Muff gave a loud miaow and gave a standing jump onto my shoulder, her favorite trick, which always makes Winchester bark, mostly out of jealousy, I think. Alexis, who is very bright, sat up on his hind legs with his front paws up, begging. That was one of the tricks the rat book said rats learned easily, and either it was absolutely true or Alexis had a rat IQ of about two hundred, because I only had to reward him twice with a nibble of cheese before he got the point. Now, whether he wants love or to be picked up or food, he begs.

"Okay, Alexis," I said, and put him on my other shoulder. "Be quiet, Win, you'll disturb the yogi." Because Win, having been pretty quiet during the entire walk, was now barking frantically. "Quiet!" I yelled again. But it was too late. I could hear the steps coming clop, clop, clop up the stairs. We're the only apartment on the top floor, so it had to be for me. Sure enough, the bell rang.

Muff leaped off my shoulder. Alexis started running down my arm. And Winchester, of course, suddenly remembered he was a guard dog and was now barking and growling.

At first it seemed to me that the smartest thing to do would be to pretend I wasn't there. So I stood still, in the middle of the hall, quietly putting Alexis into my blazer pocket, where he scrabbled around for a bit and then settled down.

The bell rang again. "I know you're there," Mrs.

Schuster yelled. "I heard you come up the stairs with the wild dog."

"What do you want?" I yelled back. "And he's not wild."

"Why can't you have a quiet dog? You know I do my meditating after work and before I go to class. You deliberately take him out then and he barks all the way downstairs and all the way up."

"He didn't bark on the way up."

"Well, he did after you got in. Right over my head. Where is your aunt? I'm going to tell her that either she makes you get rid of that dog or I'm going to tell the super."

I stood there scared and hating her. Do this, we'll take your animals. Do that, we'll have them killed . . . I knew if I said anything I'd stutter and I couldn't think of anything to say anyway.

Silence. Then, "Ya hear me, kid? Keep him quiet or I'll . . . or else!" And she went clop, clop, clop down the stairs.

It took me a minute to realize it was okay for now. "Winchester," I said, holding him by the front paws and dancing down the hall, "she's got it out of her system for now, anyway. Hurray!"

It was about half an hour later when I was busy cleaning out the cages and giving the animals fresh food and water that I heard a slight noise from the front door. I looked down the hall. A white envelope was lying on the floor just in front of the door. I went over and picked it up and recognized it immediately. It was put there by the super and was from the landlord and was one of those envelopes with the bill for the rent on the inside of the flap.

I stared at it for a minute with the beginning of that sick feeling in my stomach. Then I reminded myself that there was nothing to worry about. Lots of times Aunt Jessie had sent me down to the super with the rent in an envelope or even over to the office of the company that owned the apartment house a few blocks away. All I had to do was what, for some reason, I had been putting off: go and look in Aunt Jessie's strong box.

3

AUNT JESSIE'S STRONG BOX was in the back of her bedroom closet under a pile of newspapers and what looked like clothes she was collecting for the laundry or dry cleaners, except that I was pretty sure that the clothes stayed there as camouflage.

Once I had said to her, "You're crazy, keeping money in a box in the house, with people getting ripped off all the time."

"And who is to know that the box is here with the money in it if you don't tell them?"

It took me a while to figure out the obvious answer to that. "Well, somebody's got to know if you pay the rent and the other money in cash."

"I always say I've just come from the bank."

"But you could get mugged. Somebody might see you. Wouldn't it be better to put the money in a bank and give them a check?"

"I don't trust banks. After all, if somebody mugs me all they'll take is the money I've got on me. If I put it in the bank and the bank fails, everything can go. And we'll have nothing to live on. Nothing."

"But somebody might kill you."

"I've told you and told you, Alan. If you put your trust in the Lord you have nothing to fear."

"But you're afraid of banks."

"It says nothing in the Bible about putting your money in banks."

"But—"

"My mind's made up, Alan. And that's that."

As I kept pushing newspapers aside I realized that it was pretty lucky for me and the animals that she had this thing about banks. We'd be sunk if I had to go and try and talk the bank out of any money.

I was a little surprised that I had to keep digging. Unless the box was really small, it seemed to me that it would make more of a lump. It was a real birds' nest she had there—bits of old sheet, stockings, folded paper bags, folded newspapers, a couple of afghans. And of course I wasn't helped by Winchester, who kept whuffing behind me and standing on my shoulders as I knelt, and Muff, who kept jumping on the pile every time I moved another layer, and Alexis, who got lost altogether so that I had to stop and put him in my pocket before I could go on.

But, eventually, I got to the bottom. And there was no box.

I don't know how long I knelt there, staring into the dark corner. I could hear Winchester panting behind me, and knew that his long tongue would be hanging out. Once he put a paw on my back and gave the kind of whimper which meant, let's have a game. Muff, exhausted, lay down on a sheet that I had thrown to the other side of the closet and curled up. I could hear Wallace in his cage all the way from the other room. After a while Alexis poked his head out of my pocket, ran down my leg and onto the empty floor in the corner.

I had been so convinced that the money to take care of everything would be there that there was now just a big empty space in my head. But I could tell by the way my stomach was starting to send signals that my mind was beginning to work all right, whether I knew what it was saying or not.

Maybe it was because my head was in the closet, but I suddenly started to feel hot. Wiggling back a bit I stood up, hit a shelf and held on to the closet door handle while my head went around.

At that moment the telephone rang.

If I had been thinking straight I wouldn't have answered it, because I would have remembered that it might be Mrs. Laurence. But I didn't think. I went and answered it.

"Hello," I said.

"Hi."

"Who's this?" I knew it wasn't Mrs. Laurence and I didn't think it was the hospital. In fact, it sounded like somebody my age.

"It's me. Betsy."

"Betsy?" I couldn't believe it.

"Sure. Why not? Why shouldn't it be me?"

"What do you want?"

"You don't sound very friendly."

"Why should I be friendly? Didn't you make that crack about teacher's pet?"

"I didn't mean it to sound that way. I was joking, but it didn't come out right."

"It sure didn't. And I'm not a teacher's pet. It's just because . . ." But to talk about my stammer was as bad as stammering. "So what do you want?"

There was a silence, then Betsy said in a funny sort of a voice, "I was just wondering if you'd like to go to a movie and have a pizza afterwards. Or a soda."

I was so surprised I didn't know what to say. I just stood there holding the phone.

"Well, if you're going to be like that, I take it back," she said.

And I could tell she was mad. Or maybe not mad but hurt. Aunt Jessie sounded like that once when I didn't want a piece of the cake she'd baked.

"Look, Betsy. Don't be mad. It's just—" I couldn't think about going out to a movie with that blank space in the corner of the closet. It was like a huge thing that grew and grew.

"What's the matter?" Betsy asked.

I don't know what made me say what I did. The moment it came out I couldn't believe I'd said it. What I said was, "Something awful's just happened."

"What?"

"I can't talk about it," I said. And because I didn't know what to do, I hung up.

The telephone is in what Aunt Jessie called the parlor, that is, the room between her bedroom—what used to be her bedroom—and mine. When I hung up I just sat in the chair beside the telephone, and it was almost as though I were looking at the room for the first time. To me the apartment had always been the kitchen and bath at one end and the animals' and my room at the other. As a matter of fact, I didn't go into the parlor very much, except when I wanted to watch television, and until I'd gone into the closet, I hadn't gone into Aunt Jessie's bedroom since I'd come back from the hospital. And when I went into her bedroom, I was thinking about the strong box, not Aunt Jessie.

But now I thought about her. Some of the furniture, the chair I was sitting in, the other comfortable chair and the china display cabinet which held her collection of little jugs and porcelain figures, had come from the big apartment on Fifth Avenue where she'd worked. But the sofa and the carpet and a kind of chest had come from Scotland. Except for that corner of the bedroom closet, which was untidy on purpose, Aunt Jessie was neat. Her Toby jugs and figures in the cabinet were always in the same place, as were the things on her chest in the bedroom. Muff had broken a little blue dish jumping up on the chest one day. Aunt Jessie had clicked her false teeth, muttered something about keeping the animals in their own part of the house and put the pieces back together with glue so well that you could almost not see where it was broken.

There were pictures of her mother and father on the wall, and a huge photograph of Loch Lomond opposite.

I don't know why I suddenly was feeling terrible about Aunt Jessie, as terrible in one way as I felt about the missing strong box in another. But it was as though she were in the room, telling me that she wanted to be buried in Scotland, and I hadn't told anybody about it, and now it was too late, and I didn't know where she was.

It seemed to be a toss-up whether I would cry or throw up, when I heard feet running up the stairs and then a banging on the door.

I froze and decided if I just didn't make a sound whoever it was would go away.

There was another loud knock and Betsy's voice called, "Alan, let me in. Come on. I know you're there."

Slowly I got up and went to the door and opened it.

Betsy, who's Ms. Push, pushed in. "Alan, you look awful. What's the matter?"

"I'm going to be sick," I said. It was lucky that the bathroom was near the front door, because I only just made it.

Betsy stood in the hall while I was heaving over the toilet.

"Have you been eating a lot of junk?" she asked when I finally stood up and flushed the toilet.

I didn't think it was any of her business, but my knees felt queer and my head was light and I didn't feel up to making an issue out of it. "I don't think so."

"What did you have for lunch?"

"What everybody else had at school, a sandwich and a glass of milk."

"Did you have anything on the way home?"

"Who're you trying to be, Dr. Welby?"

"Well, there's got to be a reason why you're sick. Nobody's sick for no reason at all. Here, have some water. That'll make you feel better."

I didn't think water would do anything for me either, but I stood in the hall leaning against the wall and watched her as she went into the kitchen, opened up some cupboards, found a clean glass, opened the refrigerator, got out a lot of ice, put it in the glass and added cold water. Then she poured out some of the water and added more ice. "Now," she said, bringing it over to me, "sip this slowly."

As a matter of fact, it did make me feel better.

"This place," Betsy said, "is a mess."

I had only been alone for two days, but it was true that I had managed to use quite a few dishes and glasses and had left a lot of stuff from the cupboards—cookies, peanut butter, empty cans of dog and cat food, pack-

ages of food for the Gerbils and Wallace and Alexis—
out on the counter space, which was pretty small.

"Your aunt's not very tidy, is she?" Betsy said.

I felt irritated and guilty. Poor Aunt Jessie never
left anything out in her life. You could count on it.

"She's away," I said, not thinking.

"I thought she was busy nursing a sick friend who's
like a sister to her."

Betsy says she's going to be an investigative reporter, and sometimes when she asks questions she
sounds like she's discovered some cover-up she's about
to expose.

I couldn't think of anything to say, but it wasn't
necessary, because Betsy's always willing to talk. "Anyway," she went on, looking at me, "that's what you told
Mrs. Laurence."

"If I told it to Mrs. Laurence, how come you know
it?"

"I don't reveal my sources," Betsy said, in the kind
of voice that made me want to kick her.

"You probably don't have any, except for your big
elephant ears."

Betsy's hair spends most of the time all over her
face. Now she shook it back. Her eyes were so dark they
were like two bits of coal, shiny, with sparkling lights,
which meant she was angry. "That's a lie. It was—" she
swallowed. "Never mind. *Somebody* heard Mrs. Laurence tell The Sludge. So I do have a reliable source.
And you ought to be nice to me. I asked you to a movie,
and I came over to see if you were sick and needed

68

help, and all you do is say rotten things. You're a *noth-ing*, Alan Mac—" And then she let out a squawk. "What's that?"

Suddenly I felt much better. The future investigative reporter had me by the arm and was back against the wall staring at Alexis, who had come to see what was going on and was sitting up, begging.

"That's Alexis," I said, playing it very cool. "He hopes you have something for him to eat."

"Yeah. Like rat poison."

I jerked my arm away.

"I like Alexis a lot better than I like you. He's friendly, and he isn't always telling people what to do. And if you even *mention* rat poison in this house you can just leave."

Betsy went red and then white. "That's okay by me. When a person tries to be friendly—"

"What's friendly about talking about rat poison in front of a rat?"

"Well, I didn't know he was your pet. You never explain *anything.*" She went to the door and then turned. "And just for that I'm going to tell *everybody* that your aunt is away and you lied about her sick friend and The Sludge will hear about it. . . ."

But she didn't leave. By that time I had picked up Alexis and put him on my shoulder. "Don't," I said to Betsy. And then, although it almost killed me, but keeping my mind on the animals, I added, "Please."

She didn't move to open the door. We stood looking at each other.

69

"What's going on, Alan?"

For the past few minutes I had forgotten about the strong box not being there. But now I remembered it.

She came away from the door. "You're looking funny again."

I was feeling funny. Part of it was that I found I didn't want her to go, but nothing seemed right to say.

"What's that?" Betsy asked.

"What's what?"

"That noise?"

For a minute I didn't know what she was talking about, because I was so used to the sound.

"Oh, that's Wallace on his wheel."

"Who's Wallace?"

"My hamster."

"Let's see."

"Okay."

We started walking down the long hall, and all of a sudden it hit me that Winchester, who is usually at the front door barking his head off if anyone is there, was suspiciously quiet. And where was Muff?

But just to prove, as I've always known, that there's ESP between animals and people, at that point Winchester came bounding out of Aunt Jessie's bedroom, baying like the Hound of the Baskervilles, to make up, I supposed, for his delinquency in sleeping, or whatever he was doing when Betsy came to the door.

"Hush, be quiet," I ordered, thinking of Mrs. Schuster. I had her stopped for the moment, but who knew how long that would last? And then, "Whoa!" as he flung himself at Betsy.

Betsy had that stiff, white look again, and it made me very happy to realize she was afraid of Winchester.

"He's okay," I said. "Just friendly."

"What do you have here, a zoo?"

"Sort of. Come here, Win. Now sit down. *Sit!* Now give her your paw."

It's lucky that whenever he decides to obey, which isn't always, the beagle in Winchester triumphs over the mastiff or Great Dane or whatever creature is the other part of his ancestry. His ears curved up a bit, his behind went down on the floor and his huge paw went out. He looked like butter wouldn't melt in his mouth.

"Come on, Betsy, shake hands with him. His feelings will be hurt if you don't."

Betsy thrust her hand out, grasped Winchester's paw and shook it up and down. "Whatsa matter? You think I'm afraid or something?"

I thought she might not be so bad, after all. I liked her when she wasn't feeling so sure of herself about everything.

"No. But Winchester's large and a lot of people don't realize he's only a puppy."

"You mean he's going to get bigger?"

"Sure. And heavier. Come on, let's go look at Wallace."

Betsy stood in front of Wallace's cage for a while,

watching him on his exercise wheel. "Does he like that?"

"Sure. He loves it. Gets on it all the time."

Betsy looked at the Gerbils then.

"She's pregnant," I said.

"Then what's he doing?"

"He tries to mate every now and then, only because she's pregnant she doesn't like it."

"I should think not. He really is a sexist pig."

It was a pity, I thought, that the moment I got to liking her, Betsy started climbing on one of her platforms.

"Look," I said, "animals are animals. They do what's natural for them. You can't go around taking moral attitudes like they're people."

"Who's taking a moral attitude?"

"You are, with that sexist bit."

Betsy probably would have gotten mad all over again if Winchester, who had disappeared, hadn't suddenly whimpered and then barked. The noise came from Aunt Jessie's bedroom, so we went back there. Protruding out of the closet, with all the papers and stuff I had pulled out, was Winchester's backside. From the way he was braced and from the noises he was making, it sounded as though he thought he'd found something in a hole.

"He's sure made a mess," Betsy said, eyeing the newspapers and clothes on the floor outside the closet.

"He didn't throw those there. I did."

"Were you looking for something?"

There it was, the question that was like the cap off the bottle. If I answered that truthfully Betsy would know everything. I waited for the panicky feeling I got when The Sludge and Mrs. Laurence started poking around about Aunt Jessie, but what I felt was almost like relief. It was weird. One part of me was yelling the way it always did, *Don't trust her. Don't trust anybody.* But I knew I was going to tell her, as though I needed to get some of the load off.

"What were you looking for?" Betsy asked again.

"Aunt Jessie's strong box. She always said it was there, but it wasn't."

"What do you mean, her strong box? What's a strong box?"

"Where she keeps her money."

"You've got to be kidding. People keep money in banks."

"Aunt Jessie—doesn't trust banks. She says she keeps her money in a strong box in this closet. And I know it's there somewhere because she . . . she gives me cash to go and pay the rent and the electric bill and so on."

"She must be crazy. She could get ripped off and killed."

"I told her that. But once, in The Depression, when she had her savings in the bank, it went broke and she lost all her money. So she's more afraid of that than she is of being ripped off."

"But banks are now insured."

"I guess she doesn't know that. Or doesn't believe it. How come you know so much."

"My father told me." Betsy's father teaches at the university and her mother is an editor on one of the news magazines. So Betsy's always coming out with pieces of information that nobody else knows.

"And anyway," Betsy said, "why are you looking for your aunt's strong box?"

I could have made up something. I could have said because Aunt Jessie told me to look for it, only didn't give me the right directions; or that, since she was away from the house, I thought I'd satisfy my curiosity about it. As a matter of fact, that's the kind of explanation that Betsy would have really understood. But I didn't. I heard my voice say, "Aunt Jessie died two days ago. She had a heart attack in the street and they took her to a hospital. She told them to call me, only she didn't have any identification on her. So that when I left there, after she'd died, they didn't know where we lived."

"You mean you're living here all by yourself?"

"Yes."

"Wow! That's cool. I'd love to do that."

"You mean you wish your mother and father were dead?"

"No. But sometimes they're an awful drag. Like tonight. They think I'm at a movie with Dottie Berger."

"You mean you told them you were going to the flicks with Dottie?"

"Sure. Why not?"

"Well, it's a lie," I blurted out.

"So? Don't be such a square. Everybody lies to their parents sometimes. You have to."

"Well, I never had any parents, that I remember, anyway. So I guess I don't know."

"You haven't been going around spreading the truth about your aunt being dead, have you?"

"No."

"In fact, I wouldn't be surprised if you hadn't told quite a lot of lies yourself between now and two days ago."

"Yes."

Betsy shook her hair back. There was nothing I could say, and I expected her to close in with the final put-down. But she didn't.

"I'm not all that crazy about lying myself. But you sounded so awful on the phone I had to think of some reason to get out. I felt just terrible about what I said in class today, and I wanted to tell you how sorry I am that I said it."

"Thanks," I said, feeling embarrassed. It was funny. I'd always thought Betsy was so awful. "I thought you hated me," I said.

"I always thought you were stuck-up, with that phoney British accent and acting like nobody was good enough to talk to. And I got tired of waiting for you to be friendly to me. The other night I heard Mother say she was working on a piece about the full social implications of equal rights. Father asked her what they were —the social implications, I mean. And she said for one thing it was women not sitting around waiting to be asked. So that was when I decided to call you."

"When will your mother expect you back home?"

Betsy looked at her watch. "In about an hour."

"Won't she check with Dottie Berger's family."

"Why should she? Besides, she went to the neighborhood Community Committee meeting."

All this time Winchester was really working himself into a lather. "Come on, Win," I said. "There's nothing there." But he didn't stop and his excited whimpering got noiser than ever. Then he started barking.

"What's the barking about?" Betsy was looking over my shoulder into the closet.

"Sometimes something in him remembers that he's a hunting hound and he thinks he's found some quarry."

Winchester gave a sort of howling bark.

From the floor there came three muffled knocks.

"What's that?" Betsy asked.

"Mrs. Schuster. She hates Winchester. Says he disturbs her meditation and is always threatening to report him to the super."

Betsy was looking in the closet. "I think Winchester's found something, only I can't see it properly because it's dark. Haven't you got a light?"

There was a flashlight in one of the kitchen drawers. I went and got it and brought it back and when

Betsy had backed out of the closet I shone it in the corner.

"Let me see," Betsy said, pushing her head between me and the door frame. "It looks like Winchester has scratched up a corner of the vinyl."

"Here, take this." Handing the light to Betsy, I crawled into the closet beside Winchester, who was still pawing at something sticking up in the far corner. "Out of the way, Win. Let me see." Pushing Winchester to one side, I took the vinyl and pulled and with a ripping noise it came up. Underneath was newspaper. I pulled that out. Resting on more newspaper was a large metal box.

"I found it!" I yelled. "I found Aunt Jessie's box!"

Backing out, I brought the box back into the room.

"Open it and see how much is in it," Betsy said.

But the box was locked.

"Haven't you got her keys?" Betsy asked.

I shook my head. "I'm sure she had them with her when she left home, because she couldn't have gotten back in without them, since I'd have been in school. But her handbag must have been stolen or lost before the ambulance picked her up, because they said at the hospital that she'd no handbag or identification. I didn't think much about it at the time. All I could think of was getting away so that they wouldn't find out where I lived."

"Why are you so mad for living alone? Don't you have any other relatives?"

"No. Besides, you said you thought it was cool."

"Well, sure. Like I said, parents can be a drag. But it's not *practical.* I mean, how are you going to manage?"

"With the money in the box. If I pay the rent and Con Edison and the telephone, who's to know? And I'm just lucky that Aunt Jessie paid them all in cash and even sometimes sent me to do it."

"What'll happen if somebody finds out?"

It was like her putting her finger on some secret button that hurt. "Then they'll come here and send me away to some orphanage or foster home and they'll take all the animals away to the pound and kill them. I know. They did it with Bruce and Lana and Reverend, a cat and dog and hamster I had when Uncle Ian died. Even though I told them and told them that Aunt Jessie was coming to take me to New York and I would take the animals then. But she couldn't come right away, so they put me in a home and gassed the animals. *Now* do you understand?" The strain of the past two days must have been more than I realized or I must have been tired or something, because all of a sudden my throat felt tight and my voice sounded funny. I dropped the box on the bed. "I'm going into the kitchen to get a screwdriver or something to open the box with."

By the time I got back I had things back in line.

"Look," Betsy said, "I *do* understand. I won't tell anyone and I'll help you."

"Thanks," I said. "Thanks a lot." I was really grateful and relieved. I was also a bit anxious. When Betsy takes something on she's inclined to take it over. "Let's see if I can get this open."

"Do you know what you're doing?" Betsy asked after a minute or two.

"This is what they do on TV and in the movies."

The strong box couldn't have been that strong. After a minute it went pop and the top sprang up.

In the top was some jewelry—a watch, a couple of gold pins, three rings and a necklace. I lifted out the tray. In the bottom was money. I took it out and counted it. Then I counted it again, aloud, with Betsy watching. Then she took the money and counted it. The answer was the same every time: two hundred and twenty-three dollars.

"This is a rent-controlled building, isn't it?" Betsy asked.

I nodded.

"How much is your rent?"

"One hundred and seventy-five and twenty cents."

"And you have the other bills. This isn't going to last more than a month. If that."

In some way I felt as though Aunt Jessie had kicked a hole right through my middle.

4

"OF COURSE," Betsy said, after we had put the strong box back in the hole, covered it with newspaper and put the vinyl and the rest of the paper and clothes back on top, "you could hock the jewelry."

"How much do you suppose it would bring?"

"I don't know. But Mother once tried to sell some jewelry that had belonged to an aunt or a godmother or something, and she got like nothing."

Betsy certainly knew a lot, but it occurred to me that that didn't always make me feel better.

At that moment the telephone rang. I picked up the receiver.

"Hello."

"Hello," said Mrs. Laurence. "Is your aunt at home?"

"No," I said without thinking. I was rattled by everything that had happened and said the first thing that came into my head.

"My goodness! I hope she has some transportation back. I'm not sure it's safe for an elderly lady to be running around at this hour."

I didn't know what to say to that. Betsy was mouthing, who is it?

I put my hand over the receiver and whispered, "Mrs. Laurence."

"Is someone there with you?" Mrs. Laurence asked.

Betsy had now come over beside me and had pulled the earpiece of the phone so that she could hear what Mrs. Laurence was saying.

"No," I said, and at that point Betsy let out a stifled giggle.

I was furious. "I'm sorry," I said. "That was my dog sneezing."

"I see," she said. And the way she said it, I knew she didn't believe it.

"Please tell your aunt when she comes in that I called and ask her to call me back." And she hung up.

"Did you have to make that noise?" I said to Betsy.

"What's the big deal? She'll just think some kid is here with you. What difference does it make?"

I couldn't explain how I felt. Or rather, I wouldn't.

Betsy pushed her hair back. "Have you got a crush on her or something?"

"No. Of course not."

"I bet you do."

"Look, I don't need you around here making everything worse."

"Worse! You don't know what a big mess you're in. In a month you won't have enough money for rent or food. What's going to happen to you and your precious animals then?"

"I'll think of something. And I don't need your help. I was doing fine until you came pushing in."

"Well, you can just go on doing fine by yourself. It's time I was home, anyway. Goodbye." Betsy pulled open the front door and slammed it after her.

After she'd gone I thought about cleaning up. Why, I wasn't quite sure, but the kitchen looked twice as filled with dirty cups, glasses, plates and knives and forks. As I stood staring at them, a large cockroach came up from under the drainboard and went scuttling around over all the stuff there. Aunt Jessie always hated them and kept up a running battle with spray can and periodic visits from the exterminator. But since he couldn't use really toxic stuff because of the animals, the roaches only got discouraged or careful for a while. They didn't go away. It's always been against my principles to kill any creature. They all have their right to their piece of the ecological whole. But I found that while I didn't go into orbit over the roach running all over the plates, as Aunt Jessie would have done, I didn't

like his being there. Maybe it was because of the con-
flict I seemed to be having, or maybe I was just tired,
but I couldn't seem to get up the energy to move or do
anything about anything.

Luckily, the problem was resolved by Muff, who
must just have waked up from one of her long sleeps
and had come into the kitchen to see about dinner.
Jumping up on the drainboard, she suddenly saw the
roach. After that there weren't so many plates and
glasses to wash, because several of them crashed to the
floor and broke. Muff never caught the roach, which
went back under the drainboard where, probably, it
had a great number of friends and relations.

Finally I washed what was left of the dishes and
went to bed.

"Did you give your aunt my message?"

I looked at the corners of Mrs. Laurence's eyes.
They weren't crinkling now. In fact, I had a funny feeling she was angry with me. The thought of that sent
everything down, down.

"Yes," I said. And then had one of my inspirations.
"She was very tired when she came in and went
straight to bed. After all, she had to go out very early
in the morning. She wanted me to say she was sorry."

"Sorry about what?"

"About . . . about not calling you back." What else
was there, for heaven's sake?

"Oh. Did you tell her I wanted to talk to her?"

"Well, I left a note for her. I had to go to bed."

"But then you talked to her? When she said she was sorry?"

Not only were Mrs. Laurence's eyes not crinkling at the corner, she was frowning. All of a sudden I wondered if she couldn't be just as rigid and thou-shalt-not-ish as The Sludge.

"I told you. I l-l-l-left her a note."

Silence.

"I didn't mean to make you nervous, Alan. It's just that everything seems so odd. It's not like your aunt to cut herself off like this. I worry that she has too much on her right now. What do you think?"

"I d-d-d-don't know," I got out with a bad stutter. I moved my feet and breathed in and then out slowly. "She seems okay to me. I have to go now, Mrs. Laurence."

And before she could launch any more questions I was down the hall and into The Sludge's class. Out of the frying pan into the fire, I thought—another of my aunt's expressions.

One of the first people I saw when I got to class was Betsy. I was a little sorry for what I had said to her the night before.

"Hi," I said.

She pushed her hair back. Her dark eyes stared right through me.

I shrugged, just to let her know I didn't care, and went to my desk.

I didn't do so well in class, probably because I hadn't done the homework. I had meant to, but somehow it hadn't gotten done. It was odd, I thought, sitting there with my head down, hoping that The Sludge wouldn't call on me, that I got less done without Aunt Jessie than I did when she was there, telling me the various things I ought to be doing: "Be sure and make your bed before you go to school, Alan." "I'll wash the dishes and you dry; here's a dishtowel." "Take this list and go to the market. Here is some money. Be sure and get the right change." The bed and dishes were drags, and I often thought that was the reason I didn't get more work done. But I hadn't made my bed since I'd come back from the hospital. The dishes—what were left of them—hadn't been done until late the night before, and I had only gone shopping once. But I still hadn't done my assignment.

I was in the hall after morning classes when David Haines came up to me. I was sort of surprised and a little flattered. He's a big wheel around the school.

"Did you exercise your dog this morning like I told you?"

"Just around the block. I overslept."

"So you'll be taking him to the park this afternoon?"

"Yeah. I have to."

"Man, you're really going out to meet trouble, aren't you?"

"Those kids didn't use to be so bad."

"No. But they are now. There's going to be an all-block meeting next week to see what can be done. There are a lot of old people like Mr. Lin in the neighborhood, and they're scared to go out. People have already talked to the local precinct. It's a question of how many cops they can afford to watch the streets and the park. But I had an idea I thought I'd talk over with you. I often take Mr. Lin and his dog out and put them on the bench, then I do my jogging and come back and pick them up. Until now that's been okay. But, as you saw, it isn't now. So—you can come out with him and me. If your dog needs a lot of running, he can run with me, or you can play catch with him in the open place around the bench where Mr. Lin sits. And you can keep an eye on him."

"What do I do if those kids come up?"

"You blow a whistle I'll give you. It sounds like a police whistle and it might be enough to scare them off. In any case, I'll hear you, because I circle around a lot, and I'll get back as fast as I can."

"Stud Clancy has a knife."

"That's not surprising, knowing him. Did you see it?"

"Yes. He started to take it out when The Sl—when Mr. Laurence came up with the others. I didn't know he jogged. Mr. Laurence, I mean."

"He was quite an athlete in his day. Track, swimming, tennis. That was before he was ordained, of course. Well look, if you don't want to keep an eye on Mr. Lin, I'll find somebody else. You'll just have to run your dog up and down the avenue."

There was something in his voice that made me say quickly, "Sure I do. What time?"

"By the time I finish class and coaching, it'll be five. Say five thirty, outside my house."

"Okay."

David loped off, and I wondered what it was in his voice that was still making me feel uncomfortable. And then I knew: it was a kind of disgust, or maybe scorn. And that really depressed me, because I could see that he thought I was some kind of coward.

That afternoon I kept my head well down in class in case The Sludge called on me, but he didn't. Thinking about him in a sweat shirt, jogging, it was easy to imagine that he'd won some international prize, maybe an Olympic medal. Or maybe the men's singles at Wimbledon. I glanced up. He had on his round white collar and black front and didn't look as though he had won anything. He looked uptight and ready to pounce. I kept my head inside my book and waited until he had left the classroom before I looked up again. I still hadn't done that double assignment, and I was feeling worse about it than I did when he gave it to me.

That afternoon I got out the strong box, counted out the rent money, put it in the envelope and went downstairs to the super's apartment, which is in the basement.

I had rung twice and was about to go away when I heard his voice yell, "Who is it?"

"It's me, Alan MacGowan. I have the rent."

The door opened a little and his bare arm came out. "Okay. Give it to me."

But I remembered Aunt Jessie's training. I held on to the envelope. "I want a receipt."

I heard him mutter something. Then he said, "Wait."

A minute later he came back. The door closed again while he took off the chain, then he opened it. "So give me the bill and I'll write on it." He was standing there in white underwear and trousers, with a pen in his hand. His hair was tousled and his eyes were puffy. He must have been taking a nap.

"I'm sorry if I woke you up." What with Aunt Jessie gone, I wanted to keep on his right side so he wouldn't ask a lot of questions.

He didn't say anything, but held out his hand. I took the money out of the envelope and gave it to him, then I handed him the envelope so he could write across the bill part of it. He put the money in his pocket and put the envelope up against the wall so he could write on it. But the pen wouldn't write in that position.

He said a short four-letter word, finished writing and handed it to me. Then he said, "Mrs. Schuster's making complaints about your dog. The lease says no pets. We got the right to get rid of him if he's a nuisance. So keep him quiet."

"What do you mean, no pets?"

"Like I told you. It says so on the lease. We gotta have it so if someone has a dog or cat that bothers another tenant or messes up the house, it has to go. Mrs. Schuster says your dog barks all the time."

"It doesn't bark all the time. That's a lie. Just sometimes. Mrs. Schuster's making it up." For a minute we stared at each other. I wanted to say something else—something that would finish Mrs. Schuster for good. But I was so angry and scared I couldn't think of anything.

He gave a big belch. "I ain't seen your aunt lately. She been sick?"

"She's been helping a sick friend over on the east side."

"Yeah? Well, I ain't seen her go in or out. But tell her what I said about keeping the dog quiet."

I went back upstairs feeling rotten and worried, because I knew there was no way I could keep Winchester from barking.

That afternoon Winchester and I met David, Mr. Lin and Ming and we walked slowly to the park because neither Mr. Lin nor Ming could walk fast.

"Now," David said, when Mr. Lin was settled on a bench with Ming sitting down at his feet, "I'm taking off up there. I'll take your dog"—he gestured at Winchester—"with me if you want, or you can keep him here. Did you bring anything with you to play catch with?"

"Yeah." I pulled a ball out of my pocket. "I brought this."

"You can play ball with him, then. That'll give him exercise."

David waited for a minute, but I didn't say anything. I wanted to say, take Winchester for a run. But

I couldn't get the words out. I guess I was jealous. I didn't want Winchester running off with somebody else.

"Whatever you want," David said, and took off. Winchester, who had been scratching himself and yawning, took off after him, his ears streaming back. I wished like anything I were with them. Maybe my face showed it or something.

Mr. Lin said, "I'm sorry you can't run with them because of us."

"It's okay," I said, not really meaning it.

"If it were just me," Mr. Lin went on in that careful voice, "I would say, go on, follow them. But you see, as I told you the other day, Ming is old. He would be helpless if anyone . . . if those boys wanted to . . . to tease him. And I could not help him."

I felt ashamed then. "Look. It's okay. Really." I bounced the ball up and down in front of me and then crouched down and stroked Ming's head between his ears. "What kind of dog is he? I guess I should say, what kinds of dog?" Suddenly I remembered our conversation of the previous day. "But I guess, since he came off the street, you wouldn't know."

After a minute Ming put out a small pink tongue and licked me.

"He likes you," Mr. Lin said.

That seemed to exhaust the conversation, so I just crouched there, stroking Ming between the ears and wishing I could take off. Then I really came to attention when Mr. Lin said, "You know, I haven't seen your aunt in the past few days. I hope she isn't ill."

I looked up. "I d-d-didn't know you knew Aunt Jessie."

"Oh yes. She used to come to the park with Ming and me sometimes. And if she'd cooked meat for hamburgers or a stew she'd bring some for Ming in a paper napkin. Also, I get up early and I sit at the window and read, and I was used to seeing your aunt go out with her shopping bag to look at the fruit stalls up and down the avenue. I haven't seen her in the past few days."

"She's nursing a sick friend over on the east side," I said, producing the story that was beginning to sound less and less, rather than more, true.

"And left you alone in the house?"

"No," I replied quickly, and then wondered if it wouldn't have been better if I'd said yes. "She goes in and out at different hours."

Mr. Lin didn't say anything for a minute. Then, "It's strange that I haven't seen her. I sit at the window a lot." His narrow black eyes were looking at me from behind his thick glasses. I was feeling very uptight, because I was sure he knew I was lying and was trying to catch me out. I stood up and started bouncing the ball hard, trying to think of something—anything—to say that would get his mind off not seeing Aunt Jessie. And then he sighed and said, "Of course, my sitting at the window doesn't mean that much, since I see so poorly. I try to pretend that I don't. But I do."

It was as though a giant hand had started to un-clamp itself around my middle. Then I wondered if he was just saying that.

"Have you lived in the neighborhood long?" I asked, because I couldn't think of anything else to say.

"For almost thirty years. I used to teach at the university, you know. But I retired ten years ago, and thought then of going somewhere else to live, New England or even Florida. But my wife didn't want to move. Our friends were here. So we stayed. Then three years ago she died. Now it's too late."

Suddenly I remembered what Aunt Jessie had said: "Old people don't have any rights, either."

"Would you like to live somewhere else?"

"If it were safe, I'd be quite happy to stay here. Those of my friends who are still alive are here. I have David. And the chess club, and the university, and Mr. Laurence still sends me young people to coach, from time to time."

"The Sl—Mr. Laurence?" I said. "I didn't know you knew him?"

"I've known him most of his life. I knew his parents in China when I visited relatives there. In fact it was because his parents knew that I lived and taught in New York that they sent him to the university here. He comes and plays chess with me. Do you like him?"

The question came out of the blue and I didn't have time to prepare for it. "No," I said.

"Why not?"

As soon as I spoke I knew it wasn't true all of the

time. "He was okay the day I saw him in the park here."
That is, I thought, until he started asking me about my
aunt. And of course, if it weren't for my particular problem I wouldn't have minded that so much.

"But you don't like him at school?"

"No." And then, because he seemed to expect me
to say something, "He's different there."

Mr. Lin folded his hands around his cane. "Can you
explain how?"

I bounced the ball up and down. All I could think
of were the double assignment and The Sludge's round
white collar and black front and the sick way I felt when
I thought he was going to call on me in school and a
general feeling that was hard to describe, as though he
were on some kind of platform looking down.

"Never mind," Mr. Lin said. "I didn't mean to
press you. But when you're a teacher, it's sometimes
hard to know the effects you have on the people in the
class. I know."

"Well, he's uptight. Like he's waiting for somebody
to do something wrong."

"That's probably because he's trying too hard. He
started working with young people because—"

I was almost knocked over by Winchester. "Hey,
here's Winchester," I said. "So you came back!"

He was standing on his hind legs, his front paws on
my shoulders, barking and trying to lick me, and I was
rubbing his back and his head. "C'mon, Win, let's have
a game!"

So he and I ran to the other end of that section of

the park, where I could still see Mr. Lin and Ming, but we could play catch and retrieve. I ran back and forth with the ball with Winchester chasing me until I was winded and then I threw it for him for a while and then ran again. Nobody came to that part at all. I saw the joggers running along on the other side of the drive and they looked our way, but they kept on going, and after a while David came back and we all walked back to the block.

"I enjoyed our conversation," Mr. Lin said. "And thank you for watching over Ming and me."

"'T's okay."

"Yeah, thanks," David said. "Wanna do it tomorrow?"

"Sure. G'bye."

Winchester and I went back upstairs. Maybe Win had got rid of his excitement, because he didn't bark at all. When I got in the apartment I fed him and Muff and the other animals, cleaned out the cages and put in fresh food and water. Then I cleaned out Muff's litter pan, put in fresh litter and took the old stuff in a bag downstairs. After I got back up it suddenly occurred to me that I hadn't eaten since lunch and I hadn't eaten much the night before. For some reason, although I felt hungry for lunch at school, I didn't feel too hungry in the apartment even when it was time to eat. At least, I thought, poking around the kitchen, I didn't have to eat all those vegetables that Aunt Jessie used to put on my plate every night. I don't mind peas too much, but you could have the rest of them—beans, onions (except on hamburger), carrots, cabbage, brussels sprouts. Sometimes when Aunt Jessie talked about The Depression, I wished there were a depression on vegetables, especially cabbage and sprouts. They were worse even than spinach, which was pretty bad.

One thing about Aunt Jessie, she always kept cookies around, and milk. I opened all the boxes and cans that might have cookies in them, but they were empty. There was about a swallow left of milk and it tasted sour. There was peanut butter, but no bread. I knew I had to go out to the supermarket before it closed, which meant spending money. And just thinking about money depressed me so much that I didn't want to eat at all. I always thought that adults were obsessed about money and that was one of the things that was wrong with the world and society. But now I knew what they felt like when there wasn't enough. The thing that I couldn't figure out was, where did Aunt Jessie get her money? Of course, what I had found in the strong box might have been all that was left after we had lived on what she had for more than six months, and even if she hadn't died, we still might have had the problem of getting more. But it would have been her problem, not mine. It also might be true that she had had some regular source I didn't know anything about.

Getting the box out of its hole, I counted what was left: forty-eight dollars and change. I sat on the floor and thought. I knew there were other bills coming in, but I didn't know how much they'd be. I got out five of the dollars and thought some more. The thing was, it wasn't just food for me. The cans for Winchester and Muff were beginning to run out, and while there was still plenty of food for Alexis and Wallace and Mr. and Mrs. Gerbil, sooner or later I'd have to get more. I took out two more dollars, put them in my pants, and put the box back.

I'd never really looked at the prices in the market before, and hadn't realized they were as high as they were. There wasn't much I could do about the milk—there was only one price for that. I got the cheapest bread there was, was glad I didn't have to worry about vegetables and bought a pound of chopped chuck. I'd never actually made hamburgers, but I'd watched Uncle Ian and Aunt Jessie and cooks in hamburger joints and it didn't look too difficult. They were having some kind of a special on for peanut butter, so I bought a jar of that.

It was with the animal food that I had a problem. The kinds that Muff and Winchester were used to were there all right. But there was both cat and dog food that was cheaper. I stood there wondering what to do. Some kinds of pet foods are filled with cereal instead of meat. On the other hand there was the problem of money.

"Having trouble?" a female voice said behind me.

I swung around. There was Mrs. Laurence. I checked her eyes. They were crinkling a little, so maybe she wasn't still mad at me.

"You seem lost in thought over the dog food," she said.

It suddenly occurred to me that she might know about the difference between the brands. I knew the Laurences had some kind of a dog. "Winchester usually eats this," I said, indicating one variety. "But this is cheaper. I wonder if it's any good."

"I've never used it. Pedro, our dog, uses the kind Winchester uses. What does your aunt say?"

There it was again: your aunt. "She leaves feeding the animals up to me. I was just thinking about saving money, that's all." I decided I'd better move on, so I grabbed some cans of the more expensive kind, and went down the shelf to the cat food. "Thanks a lot," I said over my shoulder. I knew she was still there, but I concentrated on the cat food. It turned out that there was only one can of Muff's usual kind, so I took some of another cheaper brand and trundled my cart as fast as I could to the checkout counter. On the way I passed the cookie shelf. The kinds I liked were all there but, as with the dog and cat food, they were the most expensive. It occurred to me that Aunt Jessie had really laid out a lot of money to get stuff I liked, because I never saw her eat more than one or two cookies the whole time I was there. I felt a bit bad about that, because I'd always thought of her as sort of stingy, as the typical Scot is supposed to be. Taking a box of one of the kinds I liked off the shelf, I made for the cash register.

I suppose I wasn't paying attention to the figures as the girl pounded the register, but when she said,

"That'll be seven dollars and thirty-four cents," I knew I was in trouble.

"Look," I said, "I've only got seven dollars with me. Can I bring you the thirty-four cents tomorrow?"

"Sorry," the girl said, "no credit. Can't you read the sign?" And she pointed to a piece of cardboard scotch-taped onto the register. She chewed her gum and said, "What do you want to take back?"

"Never mind," Mrs. Laurence's voice said behind me. "Here—I'll pay the difference."

I don't know why that made me mad, but it did. "'T's okay," I said, snatching up the box of cookies. "I don't want this anyway." And I took it back to the shelf.

The girl took out the check and figured on it in pencil. "That'll be six seventy-one," she said.

I handed over the seven dollars, she pounded a key, the drawer flew open, and she handed me the change. Then she slowly put the stuff in a paper bag while I stood there knowing Mrs. Laurence was behind me. Finally the checkout girl had finished. "Thanks again," I muttered over my shoulder and left.

All the way home I knew I'd been rude and surly and I didn't know why.

That night I discovered that if you cook hamburger without first putting grease on the pan a lot of it sticks to the pan. I'd forgotten about the butter or margarine until almost half the hamburger I'd put in got stuck, then when I went to the refrigerator to get some I found there wasn't any. I should have got some at the market, only now it was too late. I took the pan over to the sink to get the goo out, only I forgot to cool it off under the cold water first, so when I accidentally put my hand on the bottom of the pan I gave a yell and dropped it. After I finally found a pot holder and got the pan into the sink I wasn't very hungry. If I'd had the cookies I would have eaten some, but I didn't. I thought about making myself a peanut butter and jelly sandwich, but there was a blister on my hand and the whole thing seemed too much trouble. So I played with Alexis and Wallace for a while and then went to bed.

"What's the matter with your hand?" The Sludge asked the next day, when I'd dropped the chalk for the third time.

He had sent me to the blackboard to list the kings of Israel. The burn was in the inside of my right hand, across the palm and up the first finger, and the skin was blistered and tight.

"I burned it," I said.

He gave me one of his cold, suspicious stares. The kings of Israel had been part of the double assignment that he'd given me the week before. Actually, it was because of the burn that I'd done the assignment. Either because I'd gone to bed early or because my hand was throbbing, I'd waked up early, around five o'clock. After drinking some milk and eating bread and peanut butter, there was nothing to do until around seven when I planned to take Winchester out. So, after looking through the medicine cabinet in the bathroom for something to put on my hand and finding nothing, I finally read First and Second Kings in the Old Testament, and read the text book that went along with it. Then I took Winchester out and ran for an hour in the park before going to school. David was right. There was nobody around except joggers and people with binoculars, staring at the birds. But it was really nice, cool, with mist coming off the river and the sun breaking through. Then I took Winchester home, drank some more milk, fed Winchester and Muff and went to school. A couple of hours later I was glad I'd done the work, because The Sludge called on me practically before he'd sat down. It was when I was listing the kings on the board that I started dropping the chalk.

"Let's see your hand," The Sludge said now.

I walked over and showed it to him.

"How'd you do that?"

Luckily, I'd thought of what to say if anybody asked me.

"Aunt Jessie asked me to take the frying pan over to the sink, only I didn't know she'd just been using it."

His greenish brown eyes bored into me. "I see," he said after a minute. "Did she see it this morning?"

"No. She left before I got up."

"Well, as soon as the class is over I want you to go to Mrs. Laurence and let her put something on it. It could get infected. Yes, Betsy?"

I turned quickly. Betsy's hand was waving at the back.

"Maybe Alan's aunt thinks burns shouldn't be covered."

I realized that Betsy was trying to help me out, and smiled at her across the class. She gave me a stony stare back.

"Yes," The Sludge said. "I've heard that theory. But I have a feeling that that applies where the person who's burned is in the hospital under reasonably clean conditions. Not in a school. Alan, report to Mrs. Laurence."

"How did you do it?" Mrs. Laurence asked, when I was in the office half an hour later.

I told her the same story I told The Sludge. As fiction went, it seemed to me to be okay, and after all, The Sludge had accepted it. But she paused in smearing burn ointment on my hand. "You mean your aunt called you from another room to take the frying pan?"

"No," I said, without seeing the hole that was opening up in front of me.

"Then how come you didn't know she'd been using it and that it would be hot?"

"I was doing something else," I said rather desperately. And then, with sudden inspiration, "I was at the kitchen counter, opening up cans of food for Winchester and Muff."

"So when she called you over to the stove to take the frying pan, it never occurred to you that it might have been sitting on heat and would be hot?"

"Ouch!" I yelled. She hadn't really hurt me but I wanted to get her mind off this line of investigation. It seemed to work.

"Sorry. I didn't mean to hurt you. Okay now?"

"Okay," I said through my teeth, as though the whole thing were agony.

She didn't say anything after that until she'd finished wrapping the bandage around my hand. "Now," she said, "try not to get it wet, and come back tomorrow."

"That was a dumb story you told," Betsy said after morning classes in the playground. We were all there milling around, waiting to go to lunch.

I was so glad that she was speaking to me that I decided not to get mad. "Yeah, I know, but I didn't know what else to say."

"How did you do it?"

"Trying to cook some hamburger." I told her the real version.

"It's better to use some grease," Betsy said.

"I know that now."

"But you can do without. I've seen my mother do it. You get the pan very hot and put salt on it and slap the meat down. If the meat has enough fat it won't stick."

"Thanks a lot," I said. But the whole idea of cooking turned me off.

"Does your hand hurt?"

"Yes."

"If you like, I'll come after school and help you to cook."

"After school I'm going out with David Haines and

Mr. Lin." And I told her about the old man and Ming.

"Well, I can't come after that because I have to be home for dinner."

"It's okay, I don't have to cook. I can make a sandwich."

"If you don't have a properly balanced diet you'll get sick."

"You sound like Aunt Jessie. She was always talking about a balanced diet and shoving beans and sprouts and stuff like that on my plate."

"It's a drag, but she was right. You're looking kind of washed out."

"I'm okay."

"Well, it's *your* stomach."

After lunch the whole school assembled for rehearsing the concert we were going to give at the parish fair. This was a fair given every year to raise money for the school. Of course I hadn't been there long enough to have been at one before. But I heard about it from the kids at school, and a lot of the stuff Aunt Jessie had at home was bought at the fairs—pot holders, mats, a tea cosy for the teapot, small painted wooden boxes or stands to hold letters. Most of that stuff was made at school or by people in the parish and then sold at stalls at the fair. There were various games of chance, lotteries and raffles for some expensive do-dad that a rich member of the parish—not that there were many of those—had contributed to be raffled off. This year it was a big-screen color TV, and two tickets for an all-expenses-paid round trip to the Bahamas given by somebody who worked for an airline and had somehow talked the airline into donating it. But whatever the prizes, each year the school gave a concert. This year we were to sing some ethnic folk songs and some songs by Mozart and Handel. The concert, according to tradition, always opened the fair, and was supposed to be a huge success. Although, as Betsy, who likes to be a cynic, says, since most of the audience is made up of parents, naturally they would think their darlings sang beautifully, no matter what.

Actually, I enjoyed the rehearsals more than anything else in the school. One of the songs was a Scottish song, and since I was the only one who could sing the dialect properly, I was asked to sing it solo so the others could hear. I suppose if Mrs. Laurence, who usually directed the choir, had asked me to do it ahead of time I would have been nervous, but she sprang it on me suddenly, and I found I liked doing it.

After the rehearsal, Mrs. Laurence said that since the fair was only a couple of weeks away, we'd be having rehearsals four times a week instead of the usual two, and they'd be conducted by the church organist, who would conduct at the fair.

On my way upstairs to collect Winchester before going to the park I opened the mailbox and took the mail upstairs. I didn't have time to open it, but I could see that there were bills from Con Edison and the telephone company.

After I got back from the park I fed Winchester,

opened up one of the new food cans for Muff and then looked at the bills.

I guess, in a way, I had known the reality about the money since I had looked in the strong box for the first time and counted it. After all, the facts were there: rent so much, electric, gas and telephone so much. As Betsy said, it wouldn't last a month. But somehow I had managed not to think about it. When I took the seven dollars from the forty-eight that were there, that left forty-one, and for some crazy reason it seemed a lot. When I added the two bills together now, the total came to twenty-nine dollars and sixty cents. That left eleven dollars and some change.

I sat there crosslegged on the floor of Aunt Jessie's bedroom, in front of the closet, with the box open in front of me. I took out the watch and the rings and the necklace with the locket that were in the top tray and remembered what Betsy had said about hocking them. There was a jeweler several blocks down the avenue, a tiny store with bars all over the window. Once Aunt Jessie had sent me there with a ticket to pick up her watch that had been cleaned. It had been the middle of the day and the store owner was there, because I could see him behind the counter, but the door was locked, and when I tried to get in he waved his hands in a "go away" kind of gesture. I think he thought I was one of the street kids who were always rattling the door to get him upset. I was about to go away when I remembered the ticket and held it up, and even then he came to stare at me through the door before he would open it. "I been robbed three times," he said as I walked in.

Maybe, I thought now, he'd buy the stuff. I'd try the next day.

By this time it was getting dark, so I put the box away, pulled all the things on top of it, closed the closet door and turned on the hall light.

Winchester had wolfed down his food, as usual. But Muff was sitting staring at her dish, which was still half full.

"What's the matter?" I asked.

She got up and rubbed herself against my leg and miaowed.

"So it's not your usual food. It's just as good."

Muff made that pawing-over gesture, as though to cover up the food, that cats do when they don't like what you've given them or they aren't hungry.

"Okay, maybe you'll want it later."

I then noticed on the kitchen counter another envelope, tan, that had come with the bills and that I'd forgotten about. It was one of those envelopes with a window in it and something blue inside. I'd seen it before when I'd picked up the mail for Aunt Jessie, but she'd just put it in her pocket without saying what it was.

Now I opened it. After a minute of staring at it, I realized it was a Social Security check.

A great burst of relief came over me like a huge wave. "Whoopee!" I yelled.

Winchester, who was sniffing around Muff's dinner, looked up.

"We got money, we got money, we got money," I said, and took his front paws up and danced down the hall.

5

THE PHONE RANG three times that evening. The first time it was Mrs. Laurence, wanting to speak to Aunt Jessie. I said she hadn't come in yet, and because I felt so much better because of the check, it seemed to me that what I said sounded absolutely true.

"Please ask her to call me when she comes in," Mrs. Laurence said. "Now don't forget."

"No, I won't." Even that sounded real.

The second time it was a man's voice asking if this were Alan MacGowan.

"Who's this?" I asked.

"This is Mr. Sinclair."

I could have kicked myself then for not saying right away, wrong number. Mr. Sinclair was a lawyer that

Aunt Jessie used to see sometimes, although I didn't know what about.

"You've got the wrong number," and then, to make up for the fact that I hadn't said it before, "I thought you were my father. My name is John—Howard," I suddenly added. The only name I could think of was Betsy's. And then quickly, "Goodbye." And I hung up.

The third time the phone rang, just before I was going to bed, it was Mrs. Laurence again.

"She was very tired when she got in, Mrs. Laurence," I explained. "She said she'll try to call you later."

Mrs. Laurence kind of sighed. "All right."

I decided after that that it might be better if I didn't answer the phone.

Before I went to bed I had some milk and bread and peanut butter, and ate a can of tuna fish that I found at the back of the shelf.

For some reason I wasn't as hungry as I usually am. I thought I'd never get tired of peanut butter, but I didn't even finish the sandwich. I considered getting what was left of the hamburger meat out of the refrigerator and putting some of Betsy's advice into practice, but I went to bed instead.

The next morning I went into the local bank, which opens early, to cash the check.

I went up to a man at a desk and asked him where I should go to cash it. He looked at the check. "This is made out to a Jessie Mary MacAndrews," he said.

"She's my aunt. She told me to cash it for her."

He turned the check over. "Well, she has to endorse it." He looked at me carefully. "That means, she has to sign it across the back so we can check her signature, but even if you took it back and she signed it, we couldn't give you the money for it."

"Why not?"

"Well, no offense, but we don't know that she told you to cash it. You could have . . . well, found it on the street where she might have dropped it."

I realized then that what he meant to say was that I might have stolen it.

"So how do I get it cashed? She's very busy nursing a sick friend."

"I'm afraid she'll have to find the time to come in herself. We'll cash it then, that is, if she has an account here. I'll look her up."

"Don't bother," I said, and walked out of the bank.

Considering what Aunt Jessie thought of banks, I thought it was pretty unlikely that she'd have an account there or at any other bank.

I went on to school and got Betsy aside during recess and told her about the check. "Look, you seem to know a lot about that kind of thing. Maybe you could ask your father without his knowing it was me asking. How can I get this check cashed?"

"I'll ask him," Betsy said. "Dad cashes a lot of checks at the liquor store, and Mom cashes some at the supermarket. Maybe your aunt cashes hers there. But they still mightn't cash it for you."

Since that was what I was beginning to be afraid of, I didn't feel very cheerful.

"How much money you got?" Betsy asked.

"Eleven dollars."

"What about that jewelry?"

"I thought I'd go down to that store down the avenue, you know, the one opposite the movie house."

Betsy pulled her lip. "He'll probably think you ripped it off."

"You're a big help," I said, because all of a sudden I was feeling frightened.

"No use getting mad at me. You asked me what I thought. I'm telling you."

That night, after I'd got back from the park with Winchester, I decided I'd better try to earn some money baby-sitting and taking down garbage for some of the old people around the neighborhood as I'd done before. I fed Winchester and put down Muff's dish. But Muff sniffed at the food and then walked away and sat down in the corner, where she'd been since I'd come home from school. Well, I thought, I'd better go back to the supermarket and try and get some of the food she likes.

Just to give it a whirl, I took along the check— which I'd signed with Aunt Jessie's name on the back —and asked the manager if he'd cash it.

"No Social Security checks," he said.

They were still out of Muff's regular food, so I got another kind, some milk and bread and this time bought some cookies.

I ate the cookies and some milk for dinner, then went around the neighborhood ringing doorbells where people had given me jobs before. But either they were broke or they'd found somebody else to sit with their children or take down their garbage.

"How's your aunt?" Mrs. Moscovich said, after she told me she was taking down her own garbage.

"Fine."

"I haven't seen her for a while. She been sick?"

"No, she's busy nursing a sick friend."

"Yeah? Well, she's a good, kind woman. Tell her if there's something I can do to let me know."

There was a lot Mrs. Moscovich could do, and it was all money, but I couldn't say that.

When I got home I opened up one of the new cans for Muff, but she didn't like that either. When she'd finished sniffing and pawing she went back to the corner.

"Look," I said. "I can't keep on buying cans of food that you're not going to eat. I don't have that kind of money." Muff just crouched there, looking at me out of her one blue and one green eye. Then, all of a sudden, she started making that funny, coughing noise that usually meant she was going to throw up. I got some paper under her, but all that came up was a kind of gooey liquid.

I was sorry that I'd spoken to her the way I did. "Want some milk?" I said.

I poured some in a dish and put it in front of her.

But she turned her head away. I sat beside her and tried to stroke her, but she crawled away and went under the sink. Maybe, I thought, she was trying to bring up a hairball.

Then something happened that really surprised me. Alexis, who likes to examine everything, went over to Muff. Usually Muff licks him as though he were her kitten. This time she spat and he ran away. Then she tried to throw up again.

When an animal is sick it wants to be left alone. I knew that, so I didn't go over and hold her the way I wanted to. But I sat down on the floor away from her and watched her. And it seemed to me that right in front of me she got sicker and sicker. Her fur, which was usually soft and very white, now seemed stuck together and prickly and darker. After a while I got up and fed the other animals and changed their water and cleaned out their cages, which took me longer than usual because of my hand. Mrs. Gerbil looked more pregnant than ever. She'd built a nest of shavings up in one corner of the cage which she was partly hidden under, probably to get away from Mr. Gerbil, who was at his usual activity of trying to mate with her.

By this time it was dark and I went back to look at Muff. There was no question about it: she was really sick and needed to see a vet.

Just thinking about that depressed me. The worst part was that Muff was ill, but right next to that was the fact that vets cost money. All of a sudden it seemed to me that the whole world cost money. It was something that I'd never thought about before, but now I had to think about it all the time.

The vet who'd given Win and Muff their first shots had retired so I got out the classified telephone directory and looked up names and addresses under veterinary surgeons. There were four in that general area of the west side. The trouble was, with a listing you couldn't tell who was okay and who'd do more harm than good.

After staring at the names for a while I called up Betsy.

"We use Dr. Sanders," she said.

I called up Dr. Sanders. A recording said he was away on vacation.

I called Betsy back. "Well, I don't know any other," she said. "You'll just have to cross your fingers and pick one."

I finally decided on a Dr. Stein simply because he was the nearest. But when I telephoned I got an answering service that said Dr. Stein's office would be open from eight to one the next morning.

I went back into the kitchen and looked at Muff, who suddenly started to gag and retch.

I returned to the sitting room and telephoned the next nearest vet. I got another answering service, but this one said that in an emergency I should take the animal to the animal hospital on the east side. I hung up and went back to look at Muff, who was crouched, her eyes half closed. The animal hospital was two long bus rides and a fairly long walk away. It was no big deal for me, but a journey like that would be a lot of strain on Muff. I was still in the kitchen crouched down beside Muff thinking about it when the phone rang.

I almost didn't answer it, but it was lucky I did, because it was Betsy. "Where are you taking her?" Betsy asked.

I told her what I'd found out.

"Yeah, I was thinking about the hospital. It's good but I've been there and you'd have to pay right away. Maybe a private vet would give you some time. I guess you'd better find another one."

Three calls and answering services later a man picked up the phone. "Yes?"

"Is this Dr. Harris?"

"Yes."

He sounded funny, but at least he was a person, not a recording or an answering service.

"My cat is sick. Can I bring her over?"

"The office is closed."

"But she's very sick. I'm afraid she's going to die."

"Bring her in the morning." He sounded as though either I'd waked him up or he had something in his mouth.

"But she's sick *now.*"

Pause.

"All right. Bring her over."

I didn't have a carrier, so I wrapped Muff in a towel and cradled her in my arms. I thought about taking Winchester, but I decided I'd better not divide my attention. If he took off or got into trouble I couldn't, carrying Muff, do anything about it.

It was a horrible journey. Dr. Harris's was ten blocks away, which, by myself, I could have run in five minutes. But Muff couldn't stand being joggled and every now and then gave a thin, miserable cry, and tried to struggle free of the towel.

We finally got to the house and rang the bell beside Dr. Harris's name. A buzzer sounded and the front door clicked open. His office was at the back of a long hall which smelled musty. A guy in a white coat was standing at an open door in the back.

"Are you Dr. Harris?"

"Yes. Come in."

As I brushed past him I knew why he'd sounded funny on the phone. He'd been drinking. I hung on to Muff as I looked at him. He was tall, with black and gray hair and a big arched nose. As a matter of fact I rather liked his face, but I couldn't get over the one hundred-proof odor that was blowing powerfully in my direction, or the fact that his eyes were as red as they were gray and that his white coat was dirty. But I have to say that the office and the examining room we went into looked and smelled spotless.

"All right," he said. "Put her on the table."

I was so scared that he was too drunk to know what he was doing that I almost didn't. But there wasn't much choice. So I unwrapped the towel and put her down. I don't know what happened then, but he changed: it was as though he had pushed a button marked "Sober." He leaned over her and with big, gentle hands stroked and felt her. Even his coat didn't look so messy anymore.

"What's her name?" he asked.

"Muff."

"Here. Fill out this card. Name, address, telephone, cat's name."

Muff, who was crouched and looked miserable, didn't try to get away, which said a lot about the way he was handling her. After I'd filled out the card I watched him get a thermometer and put it in her rear end. She moaned a little but didn't say much. He held it in there for a minute and then took it out.

"How much is it?" I asked.

"Hundred and five, which is high, but not as high as it sounds, because cats' normal temperature is higher than humans'."

He looked in her mouth and felt her again. "How long has she been like this?"

"Well, she didn't eat much yesterday, but I only noticed it today. She wouldn't eat, and she tried to throw up."

"Diarrhea?"

"I didn't look in her pan. And I was at school all day."

"Anybody at home notice?"

"No. My aunt—I live with my aunt—was out all day

and is out now helping a sick friend." I was beginning to feel like a recording myself.

The bloodshot eyes looked at me for a moment and then went back to Muff.

"Is it because I had to give her a different kind of food? The supermarket was out of her regular brand and I bought a cheaper one."

"What brand was that?"

I told him.

"Umm. Well, that has a lot of cereal in it, and it's true that changing her regular diet could throw her digestive system off, but I don't think it's that. She has a viral infection."

My middle felt that funny gripping sensation. "Is it serious?"

"It could be, but not necessarily. I'll give her a shot and let you have some pills you can try to get down her at home. If she isn't better, bring her back tomorrow before noon and I'll give her another shot. Now hold her for the injection."

Poor Muff was too sick to put up much of a fight, but she let out a wail as the needle went in. I stroked her and talked to her to calm her down. The doctor took out another hypodermic. "I'll give her a vitamin shot, too. That should help make her feel better."

Whatever Muff needed she was going to have, but I could almost hear the money, as in a taxi meter, clicking up.

"Okay. Here are the pills. Instructions are on the

box. Try and feed her regular baby food for the time being."

The moment I had been dreading had arrived. Slowly I wrapped the towel around Muff and picked her up.

The doctor said, "That'll be twenty dollars. Fifteen for the visit and examination, and five for the medicine."

All of a sudden he looked drunk again, leaning back against the counter as though he couldn't stand up properly.

"I came out without any money," I said.

The bloodshot eyes stared at me. "No tickey no washey. Except that you've already had the washey. So what can I do?"

"I'll bring it tomorrow." I had no idea where I was going to find it.

"Do that. Or don't come."

When I got Muff home and put her down she did seem better. Now I had to go to a market about six blocks away that stayed open until ten to get the baby food. I took five dollars out of the box and went out. All the way there I thought about Muff and I thought about money. By the time I got back I didn't feel so hot myself. I had been worried about feeling hungry, because except for peanut butter and bread there was nothing much in the house to eat. But by the time I was home it wasn't a problem. I wasn't hungry. I had fixed Muff a box in a corner of the bedroom and barricaded it in with chairs and a desk so that she wouldn't be bothered by the other animals. I now put her litter pan beside the box and her dish with some baby food in it on the other side, and was pleased to see that she wobbled out of the box and lapped some of it up. Then I went to bed.

The next morning, which was Saturday, she'd thrown up what she'd eaten and she wouldn't eat any more. And she looked just as sick as she had the day before.

Bring the money or don't come, the doctor had said.

I crouched there by the box, hating the doctor, thinking about how there should be free clinics for animals and that drunken slobs who said no tickey no washey should be put in jail.

The phone rang.

I thought it was Betsy, so I picked up the receiver. "Betsy?"

"No," a man's voice said. "How's your cat?"

"Who's this?"

"Dr. Harris."

"You said no tickey no washey, and she's a lot worse. And there should be free clinics for animals."

"Who's going to pay for the rent and the medicine?"

"I don't know. But I don't have any money and I'm afraid she's dying."

"What about the aunt you said you lived with?"

"She's not here."

Silence. "All right. I didn't think you'd be back because I was pretty sure you didn't have any money. Wrap her up and bring her in. She's going to need treatment."

Two or three times in that day and the next two (I skipped school Monday) I thought Muff wasn't going to make it. I spent all the time when I wasn't walking Winchester or taking care of the other animals watching her and making sure she wasn't bothered. Betsy called a couple of times and I told her what had happened, but for some reason didn't tell her about the vet's being a drunk. I took Muff twice a day to Dr. Harris's, where he gave her shots, and in between I poked pills down her throat and force-fed her with a mixture of strained beef and warm water. But she got worse, and by Monday evening when I was going to take her to the doctor's I was scared she was going to die. So I called him.

"I'm afraid to bring her out."

I heard him give a sort of sigh at the other end of the phone, and then something like a belch. "All right. I'll bring the stuff over. What the hell. If you're getting free office visits and medicine, you might as well have free house calls."

I didn't want him or anybody else coming into the apartment, because I was afraid that they'd know right away that no adult had been around for a while. But with Muff so sick I didn't have any choice.

"Okay," I said. "Thanks."

The buzzer rang about an hour later. I rang the

bell that released the downstairs door and heard him coming up the stairs.

When I opened the door he smelled like he did the first time I'd taken Muff to him. He hadn't so much on our other visits. But when I took him to where Muff was the same funny thing happened. When he started being a doctor he stopped being so drunk, although his hands seemed to shake a little.

"Is she going to make it?" I asked. Poor Muff, who wouldn't stay in the box, was sitting crouched under one of the chairs.

"She doesn't look too good," he said. He opened up his bag and got out a hypodermic syringe and a little bottle. Just in a few days Muff seemed to have lost half her weight. When I held her, she felt like a collection of little bones.

"If she were a little older she'd have more resistance," he said. "But she's still a kitten. Have you been getting any food down her?"

I told him about the baby food and water, which was what he'd recommended.

"Bring some of the stuff here. I've brought an eye dropper. You hold her and I'll see if we can get some more into her."

It was a messy half hour. Muff, who had looked like she was going to die an hour before, had picked up some resistance from somewhere and fought like a five-pound tiger against the soup she was being forced to swallow. In the middle the doctor said, "Do you have any liquor in the house?"

I thought he'd gone mad or was having a drunk fit. "No. Aunt Jessie doesn't approve of it. Why, do you want some?"

For the first time since I'd known him he smiled. "Always. That's my problem. But I was thinking of Muff. A little alcohol in her soup might stimulate her." He sighed. "Well, I just happen to have some on me." Pulling a bottle out of his bag, he took another eye dropper and dropped some of the whiskey into the soup. "Now let's try." Muff was on a towel in the middle of the floor. We forced the remains of the soup and alcohol down her and then stepped back. For a minute she crouched there. Then she sat up and gave a huge sneeze. After another few seconds she got her hind legs up, stood unsteadily for a minute, then wobbled off to where Winchester lay stretched out on the floor watching and slapped him across the nose.

"I think she's going to make it," Dr. Harris said.

He started putting stuff back into his bag.

"Look," I said, as I saw him putting away the whiskey bottle, "can you leave me that? Maybe I should go on giving her a little for a while."

He looked sadly at the bottle for a minute. "Bring me a glass or something, and I'll leave you some."

I got the glass and watched him carefully pour a small amount from the bottle into it.

"That's all you need for Muff."

"Are you afraid I'm going to drink it?" The minute I said that I was sorry, because he'd been so good to Muff, giving her free treatment and medicine and coming to see her. "I'm sorry. I didn't mean to. . . ." I didn't know how to finish that sentence, so my voice trailed off.

"No, I'm afraid I'll run out." He spoke calmly.

"I didn't mean to say that. You've been great to Muff. And anyway, it isn't my business."

He stood up and snapped the bag closed. "I once had a son," he said. "He'd be about your age."

"Did he die?"

"Yes. He and his mother were coming home from a visit to her parents. The car was hit by a truck. I think I'll just borrow that glass." He reached out, drank the whiskey he had poured into it, gave me back the glass and opened his bag again. "Now I'll have to give you some more. I'm sorry," he said as he poured, and his words were slurred a little, "that I took that slug in front of you. Very unelevating. I could at least have waited until I got outside."

"Is that why you drink, because of the accident? Because of your son and your wife?"

"There've been several years when I was convinced that was the reason." He stared at the bottle he was about to put away. "Excuse me." He unscrewed the top, took a swallow, stared at me, then took another. "Not elevating at all," he said, and put the bottle back in the bag.

"But you don't think that's the reason now?"

"No. That was the occasion but not the reason. Plenty of people have tragedies but don't crawl into the bottle. I drink because I'm a drunk."

"Can't you stop?"

"Maybe. I did once. I—"

The telephone rang. I knew it wasn't Betsy because I'd talked to her in the morning and she'd told me she was going to her modern dance class. Anybody else meant trouble and was pretty certain to be connected with my skipping school.

At the fourth ring the vet said, "Why don't you answer it?"

I shrugged. "If it's important they'll call back."

He stood there, one hand on his bag, which was on a table. Then he looked around my room, where we'd been working with Muff, and went over and looked at Wallace and Alexis and the Gerbils. "Your female gerbil is about to give birth at any time. You should put the male in another cage for a while."

"Yeah, I know," I said. Another cage would cost money. "Do you happen to have a free cage?" I asked, knowing that maybe I was pushing my luck too far.

He didn't say anything, but prowled back and forth between the cages. Then he said without turning around, "I have a very strong feeling that there is no aunt. In fact, crazy as it sounds, I think you're living here alone. Is that right?" And he turned.

It was weird. His eyes were still bloodshot and I could still smell the liquor, and he had had those three swallows, but he did one of his suddenly sober tricks again.

I opened my mouth to repeat my tired old story about my aunt spending all her time nursing a sick friend on the east side, but the words didn't come out. Instead, I heard myself say, "They would have taken the animals away and killed them. They did before." I must have been weak or not eaten much or tired or still worried about Muff, because my throat felt thick and my eyes started to sting. I turned my back and began to put more food in Wallace's food dish.

"That hamster's fat enough. Now turn around."

I did. He looked at me. "All right now," he said. There was something about his voice that seemed to be knocking down blocks inside me. "Now start from the beginning and tell me about it."

6

I MUST HAVE BEEN CRAZY, or, as I said, tired and strung out, because I told him everything. Or maybe it was something about the way he listened.

He didn't say anything for a while, but stood, leaning against the table, his arms folded. Then, "Does anybody else know this?"

"A friend. Betsy. A kid in my class."

"And you've run out of money?"

"Yes. Practically. Except for the check and the jewelry."

"You know if you turn up in any store with that jewelry they'll think you stole it."

"Yeah. I know."

"How much is the check worth?"

I told him.

"Well, I can cash it for you this time."

I didn't know relief could feel that way. Once again my throat felt thick and funny and my eyes stung. "Thanks," I managed to say.

"You're welcome. I'd just as soon—sooner—give it to you than the dozen or so people I owe it to."

"Do you owe a lot?"

"Yes. A lot. A great deal more than I'm worth."

"How're you going to pay?"

"I don't know. Thinking about that is one of the things I drink to get away from. But of course that's no solution. It makes it worse, not better."

"Maybe," I started to say, and then wondered if I'd got drunk on the fumes the vet was breathing out.

"Maybe what?"

"Maybe you shouldn't cash the check."

For the second time I saw him smile. "That amount wouldn't make that much difference one way or the other. And it'll hold you at least for a while. But you do know, don't you, that you can't go on this way? You're going to run out of money. And even if by some miracle you didn't, somebody's going to find out. How old are you?"

"Almost thirteen."

"How almost?"

"Well, twelve and three-quarters."

He sighed and rubbed his head. "Come to the office tomorrow and I'll have the money." Then he straightened and picked up his bag and stood a minute looking at me. "Are you eating properly?"

"No. I guess not. Mostly bread and peanut butter. I tried to cook some hamburger but got this doing it." And I held out my hand.

"That's the dirtiest-looking bandage I've ever seen. Better take it off and let me look at your hand."

The bandage was pretty loose anyway so I dropped it in the wastebasket. "Do vets know about humans?"

"We take a lot of courses in common, and a wound is a wound, a burn is a burn. Here, hold out your hand. I'm going to spray some of this stuff on it and I'll put on a fresh, smaller bandage."

"It's not as sore as it was."

"You'll live."

He started to close his bag again. Then he paused and took out the bottle.

Until now his drinking had been just funny or flaky. It hadn't bothered me. Now it bothered me. I watched him unscrew the cap. I wanted in the worst way to say "don't." But because of what he'd done for Muff, and because I liked him, I couldn't. It was his thing, and if he wanted to do it, then that's what he should do. I tried not to stare at the bottle. But it was almost impossible not to, so I went instead and looked at Mrs. Gerbil.

"Does it bother you that much?" he asked.

"It's your business," I said, still looking at the cage.

"All right. You can turn around. I didn't take a drink."

I turned. The bag was closed. "Thanks for not asking me why I don't stop."

"Is that what everybody else says?"

"Everybody else doesn't consist of very many. I'm not a bar drinker, so I don't have drinking companions. The people who used to be my friends are all thinking up ways for me to stop drinking, so I don't see them. But I'll tell you those who do make me feel bad. You do, and the few animals I still treat. I know all the time I'm working with them that they deserve better. Most people—not you—come to me because they're too cheap or too lazy to go to somebody better. I get the emergencies because I'm open late."

"You're a good vet. Muff would have died. And another vet wouldn't have let me come back if I didn't have money, and wouldn't have come here and taken care of Muff for nothing."

"Thank you for those kind words," he said lightly. "Bring Muff tomorrow morning and I'll have the money for you."

"I should go to school tomorrow. If I don't, somebody'll be up here. It's bad enough as it is. I'll have to write a note about today."

"From your aunt?"

I grinned. "Yes."

"And they don't question you?"

"Well, you see I keep telling them about her nursing a sick friend."

"Do they still believe you?"

That was what was worrying me. "I'm not sure. Sometimes I think they don't."

"You can be pretty sure they'll believe you less and less. Where do you go to school?"

"St. Alban's."

"That's unfortunate."

"Don't you think it's a good school?"

"Yes. And I like the fact that they have students of every background. But they're going to cotton on to what you're doing much faster than a big public school would. I once knew a kid who managed to stay out of public school six months, and the family never knew because the school just kept sending them letters and notices which the boy got out of the mailbox before his working parents got home. But from what I know of the Laurences—and especially if your aunt had anything to do with the parish—they're going to uncover your guilty secret a lot sooner." He looked down at me. "I'm sorry to give you all these gloomy predictions, but it seems to me a dead heat between your running out of money and somebody, probably the school, discovering your aunt's death."

His saying that made everything seem more desperate. "Well, what can I do? You know what would happen to the animals."

"That's really the guiding motive behind all this, isn't it?"

"I *told* you what happened to Bruce and Lana and Reverend."

"Yes, I know." He put his hand on my shoulder and shook it gently. "I just mean that what will happen to you, yourself, doesn't seem too high on your list of worries."

I shrugged. I hadn't thought too much about what would actually happen to me, and I had assumed it was because I didn't care much. I suddenly saw now that I cared a lot, as much maybe as I did about the animals. They'd shove me in some juvenile hall or something like that until they'd discovered they'd scraped the bottom of the barrel for my relatives. Then it would be some state institution or foster home. I found myself, for no reason at all, thinking of Aunt Jessie's body and her wanting to be buried in Scotland.

"Aunt Jessie wanted to be buried in Scotland. I don't know where they buried her. I couldn't find out because then they'd know about me. Where do they put people that have no family and no place to be buried?"

"Potter's Field. Which is another way of saying they bury them somewhere set aside for people who are not claimed and don't have money. Of the various things you have to worry about, I wouldn't worry about that."

"Do you think her soul goes marching on, the way the Church says?"

That odd, crooked smile flickered across his face.

"I don't know. But if it does, I don't think it will be preoccupied with whether her earthly body is resting out on Long Island or next to Loch Lomond."

132

"You don't? Truly?"

I hadn't thought I was worried about that. But I saw now that I was.

"No. I don't. If . . . if she's anywhere, then what she would be feeling is her love and concern for you."

Something about the way he said that made me ask, "Is that what your wife and son are feeling?"

It was weird. He'd been fine up to that moment, standing there, holding his bag, one hand at his side, sober as anything. Then he put the bag down on the table and held out his hands, which were shaking so bad they seemed to jump.

"I need a drink," he said.

"Well, take one then." I hadn't meant to sound so tough, but I was really turned off. And then I knew it was because I'd mentioned his wife and son. *Stupid*, I thought to myself. "I'm sorry I mentioned them," I said.

He clasped his hands together, holding them. "Look, don't worry about your animals. If the worst happens, I'll take them and try and find homes for them. Okay? If you have to go to school tomorrow, then either come with Muff to the office before—no, that won't do any good, I have to get the money for the check out of the bank. Come after school tomorrow. Goodbye."

He was out, with the door slamming behind him before I could thank him again.

Having the money made things a lot easier than I could have believed a month before. The vet handed it to me in two envelopes. "Put these in your shoes. It makes me nervous as hell for you to be walking around with all that cash."

"Isn't that what that traitor in the Revolutionary War did?" I asked, sitting down and taking off my sneakers. "Put Washington's plans in his shoes. Only they made him take off everything and found them. Then they shot him."

"I trust the same fate doesn't await you. Let's hope that any mugger who's looking around for prey between here and your apartment isn't up on American history. Here's an extra cage for your male gerbil. You can wrap Muff up in that towel and put her in the cage and carry her. In this cage the whole top opens. Or you can put her on your shoulder and carry this in your other hand."

We tried it both ways. Between the cage and Muff, I felt as though I were carrying a house.

He sighed. "All right. I'll walk home with you."

As I said, having the money made a lot of difference. It wasn't logical, but I started feeling surer that people believed my story about Aunt Jessie and her sick friend.

In fact, everything seemed to straighten out. Maybe, I finally decided, it was because I was feeling better. And I might have been feeling better because I was getting more to eat, or at least more meat and salad and fruit and vegetables. It wasn't that I was turning into an ace in the kitchen, it was that Dr. Harris either took me out to dinner or came and cooked dinner, at first every other night and then practically every night. When I tried to say thanks he just commented that if they tried to haul him off to jail for obstructing the state in its care of a minor, or falsely cashing checks, then he could at least enter a plea for leniency on the grounds that he had attempted to raise the standard of my diet.

"It's not," he finished, turning a steak over in the broiler, "that I have anything against peanut butter, bread and cookies, but I can't help feeling that as a steady regimen it fails most nutritional tests."

"You don't sound like the vets I've known," I said to him. "You sound more like a teacher."

"That's what my father and grandfather were, teachers. But I decided early I preferred animals to people."

"So do I. A lot. Like animals better than people."

He put the steak on a plate and started cutting it up. "Well, I'm hardly one to criticize you for that. But they can be an escape, too."

One night about a week or so later, after we'd finished eating, he looked around the kitchen and said, "It's probably because I'm not drinking, but all this squalor is getting to me. Have you cleaned the apartment or the kitchen since your aunt died?"

"Not much."

"It looks and smells that way. Where did your aunt keep her cleaning stuff?"

Cleaning with somebody else was not my idea of a fun evening, but it beat cleaning alone. Around nine thirty Dr. Harris left, suggesting that, having cleaned the apartment, I could do the same for myself in a bathtub, and then get to bed. I usually resist suggestions like that on principle, but either because something told me I'd be sore the next day, or because I felt different about him, I got into a bath almost as soon as he'd closed the door. Even so, I didn't make it to bed right afterwards. I was lying in the hot water, soaking, with my eyes closed, when Muff started to miaow. She's not that much of a talking cat, so I was a little surprised and wondered if all that cleaning activity had driven the roaches from their hiding place and she'd found one to chase. But, after a while, when she was still miaowing and, in fact, it seemed to be getting louder by the minute, I knew it couldn't be that.

"What's the matter, Muff?" I yelled.

I thought she'd be into the bathroom in a minute, since her miaowing, if it wasn't for a roach or for dinner, usually meant she wanted some personal attention. But she stayed where she was, which from the sound was down the hall by the front door, and her miaows rose and fell and rose again, getting higher and sounding like the kind of howl that I'd never heard from her before.

I got out, swiped the towel around me a couple of times and ran down the hall. Alexis was keeping a very low profile on the floor against the wall, and Winchester was sitting up with a kind of surprised look around his ears and eyebrows. One look at Muff and I could see why.

She was howling, louder than ever, and was

crouched by the door, her stomach against the floor, her backside up and her tail curving up and over to one side in a way I somehow knew, although we'd never discussed it, that Aunt Jessie would think not at all polite.

"Muff?" I said.

She rolled over on her back and gave what sounded like a great hunting cry.

"Quiet," I said. "You'll get Mrs. Schuster activated." In her own way Muff was making as much noise as Winchester did at his most excited. Maybe it was ESP or something, but Winchester at that moment gave a puzzled sort of a whimper.

"It's okay, Win." I said, but I wasn't at all sure what I meant by that. I wondered then if Muff was getting sick again. But I knew that she didn't behave at all that way when she was sick. At that moment Muff sprang and flung herself on my naked, wet feet and writhed around, moaning.

Alarm went through me like a flame. Something serious—a blockage or obstruction—could be gripping her middle and if it was that she could be dead by the morning. I ran to the telephone and called Dr. Harris's number. He answered almost immediately.

"What's the matter?" he asked, even before I could say I was upset.

"It's Muff. She must be really ill. She's writhing around on the floor and howling and twisting herself around my legs. Do you think she's got appendicitis? Do cats have appendixes?"

"No. It's not that. Tell me some more about the way she's behaving. What's she doing right now?"

"Well, she's doing this really weird thing with her tail. Her backside is up and her tail's curved up and over to one side."

"She's never done this before?"

"No. Never."

"She's about six months old, isn't she?"

"Yes. Shall I bring her over? I can get dressed."

"That won't be necessary. There's nothing wrong with Muff. She's just going into heat for the first time. I thought tonight she seemed restless and it crossed my mind that she might be working up to a heat. I meant to mention she was about ready for it, but with all our exertions it slipped my mind. I'm sorry."

"Heat!" I almost yelled. And then stopped. It was so obvious I wondered why I didn't know right away. The answer probably was that, although I'd read a lot about it, I'd never actually lived with a cat in heat. "Of course," I said. "Stupid for me not to know."

"No. It's not stupid. It can be an alarming phenomenon if you haven't seen it before."

"She's making an awful racket. I'm afraid of Mrs. Schuster downstairs. She's always complaining if Winchester even barks once. This is much worse. Is there anything I can do?"

"I'll come over tomorrow and give her an injection which will, maybe, cut the heat short. In a couple of months, you can bring her in to be spayed. Until then you and Winchester and the others will just have to be tolerant."

"I can see Mrs. Schuster's face if I said that to her. The old witch."

"Maybe she won't hear it."

But as the night wore on and Muff continued her strange howling I knew it was too good to hope for. Especially since Muff, after finally quitting around eleven, started again the next morning just as I was leaving for school.

I really worried about it off and on the rest of the day, which interfered considerably with my attention in class, and I ran almost all the way home after school before taking Winchester out to the park. Muff was at it, and I could hear her all the way up the stairs. In fact, I thought, running up, she had two distinct noises, a kind of low moan, followed by a loud yowl. I tiptoed past Mrs. Schuster's door, then bolted up the rest of the stairs, opened the door, pushed Muff back, got Winchester and his leash and was down the stairs and out again before anyone could come out and pounce on me.

But soon after we got home from the park I heard footsteps coming up the stairs, and there was a pounding on the door.

"Miss MacAndrews? Alan?"

It was the super. I stood very still, hoping he'd think the apartment was empty.

"I know you're there," he yelled. "I saw you come in with that dog. Open the door."

I opened the door a crack and stuck my nose out. "What do you want?" I asked.

"Mrs. Schuster's complaining again. She says you have a lot of cats up here howling all last night and today and she can't hear herself think."

"That's a lie. There's only one cat up here. And I can't help it if she howls. She's in heat. The vet's coming to give her a shot. She'll stop soon."

"Listen—you think I'm stupid or something? I've heard them too. There's more than one cat up here. You've got some kind of menagerie. Where's your aunt?"

"She's out."

"She's always out. Tell her I want to see her when she comes in."

"What do you want to see her about?"

"I'll tell her when I see her. And you can tell her if I don't get to see her by a week, then I'm coming into the apartment with my passkey and with the police."

"You've got no right. That's an invasion of privacy."

"It ain't an invasion of privacy if your aunt's flown the coop the way I think she has."

I just stared at him. For the first time in nearly two weeks I got that tight feeling in my stomach. "Why do you think that?" was all I could think to say.

"I ain't seen her. Nobody in the neighborhood's

seen her. And who's that man who's in your apartment at night?"

At least I could answer that. "That's Dr. Harris. He's a vet. My cat was sick. You can ask him. He lives on a Hundred and Fifth Street."

At that moment Muff, who'd been quiet, suddenly started her high and low yowling. Well, I thought, I might as well make an advantage of it. "You hear?" I said. "That's just one cat. She's right behind the door. The vet'll be around soon, and then she'll be better."

There was the sound of a door opening on the floor below.

"You keep those cats quiet up there," Mrs. Schuster yelled.

"You keep quiet," I yelled back, mad. "And anyway, there's only one cat."

"I'm going to see about that," the super said, and before I knew what he was doing, he'd pushed open the door.

I tried to stop him, but he'd caught me off guard and was inside. "You see," I said, "there's only one cat." Naturally, of course Muff chose that moment to shut up.

"I'm going to look around for the rest of the animals," the super said.

I stood in front of him. "You have no right. It's against the law without the owner's permission."

"How do you know that, kid?"

"Because my best friend's father's a lawyer." It was

a lie, but I didn't worry about that. "And he once got a super put into jail for going into a person's apartment without permission. And he'd sue you for me if you tried."

The trouble was, I could hear Wallace pounding away at his wheel, and since Alexis wasn't in his cage, he'd probably be out any moment. And Mrs. Gerbil was squeaking. I wondered if she was beginning to have her babies.

"I think you're living here by yourself with a lot of animals that are forbidden by the lease and it's against the law. I'm going to look around."

Luckily, the hall was narrow. I braced my feet against the walls. "No. You're not."

"Look, kid, I don't wanna hurt you. Now move."

He came right up to me and pushed.

I don't know what happened then. I guess maybe it was because I could hear the scratch, scratch of Alexis's feet as he came down the dark hall, and I knew that any moment the super would see him. But something got into me and I hit him with everything I had and all the science that Uncle Ian had taught me. He gave a grunt and wobbled back.

"Why you—" He came at me with a run. I ducked and butted him in the middle with my head. He gave another grunt that sounded like a squelch. Then I felt this blow on my head like a hammer from above, and for a minute I thought I'd be sick. Then, just as I was going to butt him again, I heard steps and a voice—Dr. Harris's—said, "What the hell's going on?" and suddenly the super's body wasn't over me.

"He's trying to push his way into this apartment," I yelled, before the super could say anything. "I told him it's against the law."

"The kid's lying. The aunt's split and there are a lot of animals—"

"We'll talk about this outside," Dr. Harris said firmly. He was a lot taller than the super, and bigger, so when he took the super's arm and pushed him towards the door, the super didn't have much of a chance. But he was still yelling when the door slapped shut behind them.

About ten minutes later Dr. Harris was back, ringing the doorbell.

"What did you do with him?" I asked, as I opened the door.

"Used a combination of bribes, lies and threats. It might hold him for a while, but not forever."

I looked up and automatically registered that he had not been drinking. I was beginning to be able to tell. His face was thinner, not so puffy, and his eyes were gray, not red and gray. I almost said something about it, but didn't. I wasn't sure why: maybe I thought it would be bad luck.

But a couple of days later I said, out of the blue, without thinking, "You're not drinking, are you?"

"Not at the moment. Have you done your homework for tomorrow?" He was washing the dishes, and I was drying.

"Almost. You're as bad as The Sludge."

He stopped, one hand in the soapy water. "The *who?*"

I grinned. "The Sludge. Laurence."

"Oh." He went back to washing. "Where did you get that name from?"

"I dunno. Somebody made it up. Betsy, I think. Don't you like it?"

"I've heard names I like better."

I gave a dish a couple of extra polishes. "Don't you like it when I say you're not drinking?"

He glanced down sideways at me. "I suppose I'm afraid it's tempting fate. For one thing, it doesn't mean too much. I'm a periodic, which means that I go off on toots, but then I'm dry for a while." He paused again in the washing. "Look, what I'm trying to say is this. I'd like to think that I've stopped, but I don't want you to get your hopes up. I may just be in a dry spell."

I don't know why that made me feel rotten, but it did. I picked up some dishes to put back in the cupboard.

"I'm saying, don't depend on me." There was an odd note in his voice. He sounded as though he were forcing the words out. "I'm not dependable."

"I think you are," I said. It was like crossing my fingers and making a wish.

                    *   *   *

After another week it looked as though I were getting my wish. Thanks to the shot Dr. Harris had given
her, Muff was over her heat. My homework was getting
done, and every night the vet was turning up with steak
or hamburger and making dinner. I hadn't touched
peanut butter for a week. Not that there weren't dicey
moments when I had to decide what to do. For one
thing, there was the phone. It was ringing a lot more
and I was answering it a lot less. "There's danger both
ways," Dr. Harris had said. "If you keep on answering
the phone and saying your aunt is out nursing her sick
friend, by some law of diminishing returns it's going to
sound less and less credible. Just letting the phone ring
sometimes might entail less risk. On the other hand, if
you do it too often they're going to wonder where you
are every night."

"I'll say I'm in the library, studying."

"The school library? They can check on that."

I thought for a minute. "No, there's a local branch
of the public library."

"Well, you'd better see what nights, if any, it's
open. A lot of branches are cutting down services in our
current troubles."

"I'll ask Betsy if I can say I'm studying at her
place."

"What about her parents?"

"They're out a lot. They belong to a lot of groups
and committees. Betsy said that since she turned

twelve they feel it's okay for her to be alone, at least until nine or ten. Besides, in her place, they have a doorman and security check and all that stuff."

"Do you trust Betsy?"

"Yes. She's the only one. Except you."

He flipped the end of the towel towards me like it was all a joke, but he didn't smile.

"Sure," Betsy said, when I asked her if I could say I was studying at her place. "But don't say it if you don't have to, because my parents do sometimes stay home and it might be a disaster if somebody asked them. Why don't you come over and study with me, just to make it true?"

But I didn't want to do that because of Dr. Harris. It was a lot more fun being with him. I'd already told him that I was going to be a vet when I grew up, and every night I asked him a lot of questions about animals and treating them.

One night I asked him, "Can I come and help you in your office when school's out?"

"I can't pay you, Alan. For one thing I don't have any money. For another, there are child labor laws."

"I don't want money," I said. I was really pissed off that he'd said that.

"All right," he said, "I'm sorry. Maybe sometime later."

"Forget it."

"Look, Alan—" He was wiping off the table with a

wet sponge. "I meant that about later. Just don't push me too much right now."

Afterwards, when everything crashed, I saw it was a warning. But I guess I didn't want to see it then. So I went on being silent, like I was mad. Finally, when he was leaving, he said casually, "Okay. Come around after you've done your homework tomorrow. You can help me for a couple of hours before the office closes."

"Not if you'd rather not," I said.

"Don't be a pain in the rump, Alan. Come, if you want to come. If you don't—then don't."

Of course I did, so I cut short my time with David and Mr. Lin and, with Winchester galloping beside me, practically ran all the way to Dr. Harris's office.

It was great working with him. I learned how to hold dogs and cats while he gave injections and cut nails and got pills down their throats. He showed me how to scrub down the examining table and sterilize the instruments and order supplies.

"I guess," I said as I made out an order, "you must have money now, ordering all these things."

He didn't answer for a minute. Then he said, "I have to send a check. My credit's shot. They're not about to let me charge anything."

"The creeps. That's business for you. Always charge the most you can but don't let anybody else charge anything."

"I hate to tamper with those excellent sentiments, but justice makes me point out that they have reason not to trust me. When I've been drinking I've let bills go for months."

"But you paid them."

"Eventually. Lately I've worked more so I've earned more."

The truth was, I didn't want to think about him as a drunk, so I didn't. "Yeah, but you're not drinking. And that's great."

My aunt didn't get much mail. There was a letter once from an old friend in Scotland. The handwriting was so difficult I couldn't read it, so I just stuck it onto the desk. Then there was a letter from Mr. Sinclair, the lawyer. I opened that and read that he had tried to call her several times but once got the wrong number (I remembered that!) and the other times got no answer. He had something he wanted to discuss with her and would she call him to make an appointment.

I asked Dr. Harris what I should do.

He looked at the letter. "Nothing. That might inspire him to come up here or send for the police, but if you try and answer it yourself, I think the risk is greater."

I hadn't written the note about my Monday absence nearly three weeks before when Muff had been sick, thinking that maybe this time I could get away with just telling them if they asked me. I even hoped that they'd forget to ask. But, as Betsy says about practically everything, fat chance.

"Alan," The Sludge said after history class one day, "where's the note about your absence?"

"I had to take my cat, Muff, to the vet."

"And it took all day?"

"Well, she was very sick. I couldn't leave her alone after bringing her home from the vet. She had to have medicine all during the day."

"And what did your aunt say when you told her you hadn't been to school?"

I should have thought of that, I realized. "She said that animals had their rights, too," I lied valiantly.

"That's odd, in view of something else your aunt was given to saying from time to time." He paused. "I forget the exact words, which I couldn't pronounce the way she did anyway, but they were to the general effect that she was appalled at how young people today used any excuse—large or small, true or false—to stay at home from school. Haven't you heard her say that?"

I had, and wanted to kick myself for having forgotten it. Aunt Jessie had been brought up on a moor near a West Highland village, where people seemed to go to school—at least according to Aunt Jessie—through eight-foot snowdrifts and even if every member of the family was dying. She said the way kids over here stayed out of school at the slightest excuse, the next generation of Americans would not be able to read or write.

"It was because Muff was so sick," I said, beginning to shift my feet.

"Which veterinarian did you go to this time?"

"Dr. Harris."

"The only vet named Harris we know is in the process of drinking himself out of his profession."

"That's not true!" I yelled like the idiot I was. The anger was a great fire inside me, spewing the words out.

"I see that your vet is our Dr. Harris," The Sludge said after a minute. "Why are you looking so red?"

It seemed safe enough to say, "Well, he saved my cat's life. He's a good doctor."

"I didn't say he wasn't. In fact, until his professional life started interfering with his drinking, and therefore had to be abandoned, he was the best vet I knew and we always went to him."

"Well, he isn't drinking now."

"Do you know," The Sludge said after a few seconds, "that's the first time I've known you to show enthusiasm for anything that went on two legs instead of four. I won't incur your wrath again by saying I wish it were directed towards a more . . . reliable . . . object, because who knows why or how these things happen or with what result? All right, Alan, there's no need for you to look so hot and bothered."

I was still furious, too furious to care about what I said. So angry I even forgot to stammer.

"You sound so . . . stuffy."

This time he was the one to go red. I waited for the ax to fall. Instead he said, "I suppose I do. But, you see he—Never mind. You're right. I shouldn't have said it."

"Can I go now?"

"Yes. You can go."

It wasn't until later, when we were in the middle of rehearsing for the concert—which we were doing now all afternoon, every afternoon—that I realized the question of my taking Muff to the vet instead of being in school had been shelved. This cheered me up so much that in the middle of singing a note, I broke into a giggle.

"What was that? Who made that noise?" the church organist, who was now conducting the choir, said. With the concert two days away he was getting more uptight with every rehearsal. "You'd think," Betsy once commented disgustedly, "the way he was pounding the music stand with his baton, that he thought we were the Philharmonic Chorus, instead of a tacky little school choir, and that he was Eugene Ormandy." Now he looked furiously around. Nobody said anything. "All right. If you want to sound like a bunch of tone-deaf barbarians." Silence. He glared at us. I knew the kids on either side of me knew who had made that noise, but I stared back as straight forward as anyone. "All right," he said, again, "but the next time, I'll—"

But that was a paper tiger that wouldn't fight. What could he do to us? Nothing. He needed us much more than we needed him. And it was probably some kind of tribute to his bullying powers that we only remembered that some of the time.

He gave the music stand a terrific whack. "Now, on the count of four! One, two, three, *four*—" And we were off.

That afternoon, while David was off jogging, I finished playing catch with Winchester and decided that since the gang had not turned up in this part of the park lately, Mr. Lin and Ming would be okay if I cut out and went over to Dr. Harris's office a bit early.

"I'm sure you'll be okay," I said to Mr. Lin.

He looked a little anxious. "It's just that Ming—But I am being selfish, taking up not only David's time but yours."

I didn't know why I was so bugged about getting to the vet's right away, but it was a feeling that had been growing since The Sludge had made his poisonous comments about Dr. Harris's drinking. I knew he wasn't drinking now, but I felt it was terribly urgent to get over there. I squatted down and stroked Ming between the ears and down his back. His eyes were a bit milky, and I wondered how much he could see.

"Ming'll be fine," I said. "David'll be back in a minute."

I got up, put the ball in my pocket and whistled for Winchester.

But when Winchester and I got to the vet's and I rang the bell there was no answer. I rang again. Still no answer. I rang it a third time, but there was no doubt about it, he wasn't there. There was nothing to do but wait, so I sat down on the steps. After a while I got up again; the warm weather hadn't arrived yet and it had been raining. Then I looked around for Winchester. He was way down the street. I whistled for him and he came loping back, his hound ears streaming behind him.

After what felt like another long while—I'd forgotten to wind my watch, so I didn't actually know how long it was—I decided Winchester and I might as well walk around the block. I put his leash on, and we walked two blocks down, one across and two blocks back up again. Figuring Dr. Harris might have come in while we were gone, I rang the bell again. But there was still no answer. I suppose that was when I started getting mad. Or maybe it was because I was feeling a little guilty over Mr. Lin and Ming. When I'd talked to him the day before, Dr. Harris hadn't said that he was going to be late. He'd always been there before. His office hours began at least an hour before I got there and didn't end until two hours after that. After walking up and down the block for a bit, I went back and rang all the other bells for apartments on the first floor.

There was a raucous squawking from the intercom that was just above my head.

"What?" I yelled.

More squawking.

"I can't hear you," I yelled even louder.

Whoever it was finally buzzed, the door clicked open and I got Winchester and me in before they changed their minds.

"Whaddya want?" Somebody yelled from down the hall.

"Dr. Harris," I said.

"Wyncha ring the right bell while you're about it?"

The door slammed. I couldn't tell whether it was a male or female. From the voice it could have been either.

I went down the hall to the office door, rang the apartment bell, knocked and tried the handle of the door.

It was while I was doing this that I heard the front door of the building open. When I turned I saw it was Dr. Harris.

When he saw me he said abruptly, "How did you get in?"

I don't know why I said what I did next. I didn't even know I was thinking the words. I said, "I thought you might have started drinking again." And I knew the moment I'd said it that that was what had been bugging me all day, ever since The Sludge had said his piece.

He was now beside me, taking out his key. "Thanks for the vote of confidence." His voice, as well as the words, bit.

"Well, you said you were a . . . a periodic. And when The Sludge said about your drinking—"

He pushed the door open and turned, towering over me. "You mean you and that sanctimonious prig have been having a nice little chat about my alcoholism?"

"No." Everything was going wrong. I hadn't meant to say any of this. "At least—he said something lous—something unpleasant about you and I got mad and stuck up for you—"

"Damn nice of you. But you just came to check to make sure."

We were inside by now and he had turned on the light. He looked terrible, grayish, with lines I hadn't noticed before. "What's the matter?" I asked. Then I gasped, because when he took off his jacket he was covered with blood.

"What happened? I'll tell you what happened. A criminal idiot, who had enough evidence to have called me—or any vet—a week ago, finally screeched into the telephone that her dog was dying and she couldn't move her and would I come. Well, she was right about one thing: the dog was dying. So I delivered the puppies, all of them dead, while the poor little bitch hemorrhaged her life away. There was nothing I could do. When I asked her why the hell she didn't call somebody sooner, she said she wasn't absolutely sure the dog was having trouble—even though she hadn't eaten in nearly a week and had been whimpering and throwing up—and she didn't like to waste the money. While she was telling me this I was walking down the hall of her five-room apartment and she was talking, blowing liquor all over my face, and all I wanted to do was to tell her to give it to me first-hand, not second. And when I get back you wonder if I've been out on a bender. No, but it sounds like a great idea."

"Look, I'm sorry. I got here early and you weren't there—"

"I thought you were supposed to keep an eye on that aging Mr. Whatsis and his aging dog."

"Yes, but there hasn't been any trouble lately, and I'm sorry again, but I was thinking about what Laurence said, so I left the park early—"

"Dropping your responsibility to come here and make sure I was living up to mine."

That really got under my skin. Vaguely I noticed that his hands were jumping around worse than I'd seen them before and there seemed to be some kind of a tic around his left eye. But I was too upset and angry to think about it.

"Well, at least I knew *I* wasn't going on a bender," I yelled. "C'mon, Win!"

Yanking Win by his collar I got him out the door and slammed it behind me.

7

I FELT REALLY ROTTEN for the rest of that evening, and for once I answered the telephone every time it rang, thinking it might be Dr. Harris saying he was sorry. But it wasn't. The first two times it was women from the church who wanted to talk to Aunt Jessie. I said my usual thing about her being out. The third time a man with an English accent asked if this were the residence of Miss MacAndrews. I don't know what made me do it, but I yelled,"Wrong number," and slammed down the phone. Then I stood beside the phone trying to stop the shaking inside. There was something about that call that made me feel everything was closing in, getting nearer. Maybe it was the English accent.

The next morning on my way to school I saw David

Haines come out of his house across the street. "Hi," I yelled.

He turned, saw me and stood staring. "What's the matter?"

"You rotten punk," he said. "You couldn't wait, you couldn't keep your side of the deal. You couldn't even give a blast on the whistle to let me know you were leaving. You just split because you had something you wanted to do."

My heart seemed to stop. "Did something happen to Ming or Mr. Lin?"

"By the time Stud and Lee finished having fun with Ming, throwing him from one to the other just to tease the old man—they'd already robbed him of the six dollars he had on him—Ming was nearly dead. They also beat up Lin, just for the hell of it. If some of the joggers hadn't heard both the dog and the old man scream and alerted the cops, they'd both be dead." And he turned and took off down the street.

I went on to school; I couldn't think of anything else to do. I didn't speak to anybody, but then I practically never do, anyway. Betsy said to me once, "Are you okay?"

"Yes," I replied. "Why?"

"You look funny."

"Not as funny as you look."

"Okay, wise guy."

At the end of English Mrs. Laurence kept me behind. I knew another question about Aunt Jessie was about to come up, so I waited to dish out the same old story.

"Alan, I'm worried about your aunt. It's been nearly a month now. I've tried to call. I've left messages with you. I've even been by during the day and rung your bell. I have a very strong feeling that something's not right."

I just stared at her. I was waiting for her to say, Did your aunt die and are you living alone? And I would have said, Yes. But she didn't. She said more sharply, "Alan, are you all right?" Which I thought was a funny question in view of the fact that I was sure that David must have told everybody about how I had let Ming get killed. In fact, I decided she was trying to trap me, so I said, "Sure."

I don't know whether she would have taken that, but some kid from the second grade came in all excited and said something was happening and she was wanted right away. So while she was trying to find out what had happened, I slid out.

"Alan!" I heard her call behind me. But I ran on.

I knew that Mr. Lin and Ming wouldn't be going to the park, but even though it got later and later I stood by the window and waited until I saw David take off in his jogging outfit. Then I waited another twenty minutes to be sure not to run into him. All this time Winchester had been whimpering, barking and scrabbling at the door. I should have realized that poor old Win, who hadn't been out since before breakfast, was ready to burst. He wasn't the best-trained dog in the world—after all, I'd house-trained him. Before that he was a stray. Some dogs, usually highly bred ones that are house-broken by people skilled in dog-obedience, are so thoroughly programmed that some of them will get bladder trouble sooner than do something in the house. But Win wasn't one of them. Just as we got to the bottom of the stairs, and just as the super was coming in the front door, Win lifted his leg against a door.

The super was carrying a long umbrella. With a screech he raised it and brought it down on poor Win's backside. Win gave a terrible yelp and ran out the open door while I was wrestling with the super. I got his umbrella and started beating him as hard as I could.

I heard Win still yelping outside and then the sound of a car and the squeal of brakes.

When I got outside Win was lying in the road beside a car and a man was bending over him. Behind was another car, honking.

I bent over Win, and the awful part was that all I could think of was that I knew it would happen.

"I'm sorry. Is he yours? I just didn't see him. He ran out so fast. I'm really sorry." It was the man from the car that knocked Win down.

I was stroking Win's head, thinking he was dead, but he moved a little.

"Look," the man said. "He's alive. Let's get him to a vet. I'll take you in that car. I have a dog myself. Do you know a vet? Why doesn't that guy shut up?" This was about the man in back who was leaning on the horn. "I'll go and tell him to back up and go up the drive to another street. There's no way I can move the car without moving the dog, and I'm not about to move him for that jerk." And he went off. But even though Win had moved, he didn't look very alive. I heard loud voices, then the other car went into reverse and backed down the hill towards the drive.

"Okay," the man said, coming back towards us, "tell me where I can take him to a vet."

I don't know what made me say, "Stay with him here and I'll go up and phone and see if he's still in his office." But when, upstairs, the phone in Dr. Harris's office rang and rang, I wasn't surprised. I then got out the list of vets and called Dr. Sanders again. He must have come back from vacation because somebody answered and said yes, the doctor was still in his office and bring the dog around, but be sure to move him carefully.

The guy in the car had handled Win very well. I'd brought down a blanket and we'd slid it under him and held it tight, so that we could put poor Win in practically the same position on the back seat. And I sat on the floor and held him there.

Dr. Sanders's office was on One Hundred and Tenth Street and was much grander than Dr. Harris's.

Dr. Sanders, a heavy, silent sort of a guy, handled Win gently while we stood there.

"Do you know where the car hit him?" he asked the man once. "What part of his body?"

"In front. He was running into the road, yelping, and he ran right into the car."

"What was he yelping about?"

I answered that. "Because the super hit him with his umbrella for peeing in the hallway."

"Isn't he house-broken?"

"Yes." Pause. "You see, I'd—I'd waited too long to take him out. It wasn't his fault."

"Shouldn't do that. It's bad for the dog. I've known dogs to develop permanent kidney damage from not being taken out soon enough or often enough. Who owns this dog?"

"I do."

The doctor grunted. Then he went over, washed his hands and came back drying them. "Well, he seems to have a concussion. Whether he's injured internally and how much I won't know until I've X-rayed him. Leave him here and I'll call you as soon as I know. Fill out this card."

Printed on top of the card, under the vet's name and address, was the statement: *Animals must be paid for in full before they may be taken home.* I filled out the card.

"How much do you think it's going to cost?" I asked, handing the card back.

"I can't tell you that until I know what I have to do. If he's internally injured, and it's fixable, then I'll operate."

162

"How much will that be?" the man beside me asked. "I'm on my way out of town and I'd like to leave a check with this kid here. It's my fault."

I knew this guy was being very decent and that I should say so, because he must be feeling rotten. But I couldn't think of anything to say. And anyway, I didn't want to.

"I can't tell you that until I know," the vet said. "But maybe a hundred and fifty, maybe more with post-operative care."

"Okay," the man said.

"Do you think he's going to get better?" I asked the vet.

"I can't really say until I've X-rayed him. He's not doing too well right now."

When we got back to the house the man took out his checkbook. "Look," he said, "I'm going to give you a check for two hundred dollars. If it's more, call me at home—I'll give you the telephone number—and I'll shoot off some more. What's your name?"

"Alan MacGowan."

"Spell MacGowan."

I did.

"I take it you can get your aunt to cash this for you?"

I took the check and looked at it. "Yes."

He gave me a card with his name—Jonathan Rosenfeld—and telephone number on it.

"Again, I'm really sorry. I sure hope he makes it."

I nodded. "Thanks," I said. Then I got out and he drove off.

When I got into the house the super, who must have been watching for me, came bounding out of his apartment. "I'm going to see the house owner and have you evicted if you don't get rid of that dog. It smelled up the entire hallway. I had to scrub it with disinfectant."

"You smell worse," I said, and went up the stairs while he screamed at me from below. I didn't care what he said or did.

The vet didn't call that night. The two ladies from the church called again, and Mrs. Laurence phoned, wanting to know again, one, if my aunt was in, and two, if I was okay.

I told her my aunt had come in and gone to bed and didn't want to be disturbed because she was very tired. And that I was fine.

She didn't seem to believe me.

She said, "Look, Alan. I want you to tell your aunt that I'm coming over the day after tomorrow in the afternoon and I would like her to arrange to be there. That's the day after the concert. And if she's not there, then I'm going to get in touch with the authorities. I know you keep telling me that everything is all right, but I keep having the feeling that it isn't."

"All right," I said, "I'll tell her."

I had made up my mind that I was going to stay home the next day, concert or no concert, and wait for the vet's call. But he called me before it was time to leave for school, and said that he was going to operate right away. That if he did, Winchester had an outside chance. And could he please speak to my aunt.

I told him that she'd given me full authority for it.

"I'm afraid," the vet said, "that it's going to be expensive."

"It's okay. I have the money. I'll bring it to you right now if you want." I did have some money from the check Dr. Harris had cashed. But, after buying supplies, not enough, and in a couple of days there was going to be rent. But I had the check the man in the car had given me.

"Well," Dr. Sanders said, "if you have it you can make a deposit. Come by this evening or tomorrow morning, and I can tell you how he's getting along."

So I went to school and the concert after all, and that's where I did that crazy thing.

The fair opened at five with a short talk from Mr. Laurence, the rector, and then there was the concert. The choir sang pretty well and I even had a solo song in the middle. I stepped out a little in front of the others and sang *The Hieland Lad* and I got so much applause that the choirmaster nodded to me to do the encore, *Just a wee doch an dorus,* because, he said, it had more dialect than any of the other songs I knew and people would like it. He was right. When I got to the words, "If ye ken say it's a braw bricht moonlict nicht, it's alricht, ye ken," people laughed and stamped and clapped. The choirmaster said he thought it might add another ten dollars to the collection that would be taken up. There were quite a lot of people there, practically everybody from the parish and more from the neighborhood. It was nice. Even with my thinking about Ming and Winchester it was nice, but not very important. And it was all happening far away. In the middle of one of my songs I saw David Haines standing at the back with one of the collection baskets, and I was sure that all he could think about was that I had left Ming to be thrown between Stud and Lee. I almost lost the note then, but I looked away and managed not to. I don't think anybody noticed. One of the funny things is that I can sing in public without stammering or even feeling nervous. But if I were asked to speak or recite I'd stick at every word.

When the singing was over the collection baskets were passed. David emptied them into his big one, and came towards the door between the parish hall and the church offices where we were filing out. As the soloist, I was at the end of the line and was the last out.

David was about to follow me when The Sludge, who was talking to some people in the hall, called. David looked back, hesitated, then said to me, "Here, take this basket to the rector's office and stick with it until I come, I'll be there in a minute." And he pushed the basket at me.

I went to the rector's office, put the basket on the desk and stared at the money. In a minute David was there.

"How much is there?" I asked.

"I'm going to count it now. Here, you count the

change." And he took the bills out of the basket and pushed it at me. When we added it all together it came to over one hundred and thirty-four dollars.

"That's pretty good," David said. "Better than last year."

"I'm sorry about Ming," I said. "And about Mr. Lin. But especially about Ming being killed."

"I didn't say he was killed. I said he almost was. He must be a tough little dog. He's going to be okay. I'm sorry I chewed you out, but if there's anything that turns me off it's somebody who says he'll do something and then doesn't do it." He reached out and gave me a slight whack on the arm. "If you can't do something, say so."

I felt better, a whole lot better, than I had since it happened. Maybe I didn't mess up so bad after all. If Ming was getting better, then that meant Winchester would probably get better.

"Thanks," I said. "Thanks for telling me. Can I come out in the park again with you and Mr. Lin and Ming? That is, as soon as Win's okay."

"What's wrong with Winchester?"

I told him.

"That's too bad. Sure. But, like I said, if you have to leave early, say so."

"Yes. I will. Is Mr. Lin okay?"

"He was shook up some and is thinking of moving to some place like Florida. But with Ming better, he's better. I don't know what's best for him to do. Those two thugs were taken off to the precinct by the cops, but they'll probably be back on the street again before you know it. And Lin's going to get *less* able to take care of himself on the street, not *more*. I don't know what he'll do."

I thought about Aunt Jessie's saying the old didn't have any rights either and told David.

"Yeah, well, she's right. That's one of the things that's going to have to be changed." I knew David wanted to go into politics after college. "Let's put the money in an envelope and in the bottom drawer here until Laurence can come and put it in the safe."

I watched him stack the bills, put a rubber band around them and put them in a manila envelope along with the coins. Then he put the envelope under other stuff in the bottom of the desk drawer, closed the drawer, took a key from inside the *Book of Common Prayer* that was on the desk, locked the middle drawer of the desk and put the key back.

"Okay," David said. "Why don't you go on back to the fair and enjoy yourself."

"Sure," I said.

But as soon as I got back to the parish hall, where people were milling around the booths, I left. Normally I would have stayed, but for one thing I didn't have any money to spend, and for another there was something I had to do.

As soon as I got home I fed Muff, who was now well, wrapping herself around my legs and eating like there was no tomorrow. I fed Alexis, Wallace and Mr. and Mrs. Gerbil—who still hadn't had her babies—and gave them fresh water in their aquarium bottles. Then I went to the telephone to call Dr. Harris, but decided instead just to go over there with the check. It wasn't his fault he'd been out when Winchester was knocked down. He was probably out on a house call, the way he had been when I had stupidly told him about what Mr. Laurence had said. Now that Ming was all right, and Winchester was going to be all right, I was somehow sure that everything was going to be all right between Dr. Harris and me. But it would be better, I decided, just to go over without telephoning. And if he was not there I'd wait. I was sure that when I told him what had happened to Winchester he'd cash my check.

I ran all the way. But when I rang Dr. Harris's bell there was no answer. I just stood there at the apartment house door, which had glass panels, and after a few minutes it occurred to me that the light I could dimly see through all the design and frosting on the glass came from the back apartment, the one facing the front door, which was Dr. Harris's. I stared at it for a few seconds, my face pressed against the glass. Then I rang about six bells. Sure enough, some idiot let me in without checking who I was—the kind of thing Aunt Jessie told me never, never to do. But I was glad now that somebody had done it. As soon as I was in I could see that the light did come from Dr. Harris's apartment, and the reason I could see it was that the apartment door was half open.

I ran down the hall, paused at the door, called, "Dr. Harris? It's me, Alan." But there was no reply, at least not at first. Then I heard a kind of a mumble.

"Dr. Harris?"

What I heard then I couldn't believe: It sounded like somebody snoring. I stood there for another minute. I felt afraid and I was shivering a little. Then I pushed open the door and walked in.

He was lying on the sofa in the waiting room. His face was red, his mouth was open. He hadn't shaved. An empty bottle was lying on the floor beside him. The smell was terrible.

I stood there looking at him for a minute. Then I left.

Everybody was at the fair. There was nobody in the rector's office. I took the key out of the *Book of Common Prayer,* unlocked the middle drawer and got out the envelope from beneath some boxes of typing paper. I left the coins but I took the bills and put the envelope and the key back. I kept wondering if somebody would come in, and the funny part was I really didn't care. But nobody did. So I put the money in my sneakers and walked back through the parish hall. When I got outside I looked at my watch. There was just time to get home for the rest of the money and bring it to Dr. Sanders.

Win was better, the vet said. He thought he'd pull through. He watched me while I took off my sneakers.

"That's a funny place to keep money," he said, "but I suppose the way the streets are today it makes sense." At least, I thought, Win would be all right now, no matter what happened. "How much is the whole thing?" I asked.

"You don't have to pay it now. I told you. Just a deposit."

"I want to pay it now."

"Well, I'm not sure whether your dog—Winchester—should be here four or five days, but let's say one hundred and seventy-five. If it's more I can let you know when you take him home."

I handed over the money.

"Could you take a cat, a white rat, a hamster and two gerbils, one of them pregnant, in case . . . in case anything happens."

"What's going to happen? What do you mean?"

"Nothing."

The vet was looking at me in a funny, questioning way.

"I might have to go away," I said. "My aunt's sick. She may not be able to take care of me much longer." I could hardly say, I've just stolen a large sum of money and will probably be arrested and all my animals killed. But thinking up lies was, along with everything else that was going on, just something extra I had to think about.

"Oh," he said. "I'm sorry to hear it." Then, "Look, I'm sorry, too, about your cat and hamster and the other pets, but I just don't have the facilities to keep them. Have you tried all your friends?"

I shook my head.

"Well, try them. If you're stuck there are even a couple of pet stores on the avenue that might find homes for them for you. Although I'm not too much in favor of most pet shops. Try your friends."

Everything looked pretty bleak, but there wasn't anything more I could say about that. Then I asked, "Can I see Winchester?"

"All right. I'll take you back and you can look at him. But don't talk to him. He'll want to leave with you and, when he can't and you have to go, he'll be upset. Okay?"

I nodded.

Poor Win looked awfully long and thin and flat lying there. All of a sudden I wanted very much to cry, but went back down the hall and tried to think about something else.

"Are you sure he's going to be all right?" I asked the vet after I was sure my voice would work properly.

"No. I can't give you an iron-bound guarantee. But he came through the anesthetic and the operation well and I think so."

"Can I call you tomorrow? Just to check on him?"

"Sure."

I went back home and made certain of locking the door and putting the chain on. I had to think. Then I turned off the light in the hall so it wouldn't shine under the door. I didn't know what was going to happen, but

I might want people to think I wasn't home. I went into the kitchen and thought about eating something. I even got out the bread and peanut butter, but put them away again. I wasn't hungry.

Then I went into the living room, turned on the television with the sound low and sat down. After a while Muff jumped into my lap and Alexis climbed up my leg, then up my arm, and settled down on my shoulder. I could hear Wallace pounding away at his wheel and both Mr. and Mrs. Gerbil squeaking. And I wondered if in one day or two they'd be taken away and gassed because I would be in juvenile hall for stealing The Sludge's collection. The thing was, if he didn't know already that the money was gone, he soon would. The fair lasted until nine. He might wait until the rest of the money from the stalls was counted and put the whole lot in the safe. But the more I thought, the more I saw that it was a choice of letting the pound take away the animals or turning them loose on the streets or in the park. And both meant they'd die.

I put Muff off my lap and Alexis down on the floor. I couldn't sit still. So I walked around the apartment, in one room and out and down the hall. What a dumb thing it was to take that money, but if I hadn't, I might never have been able to pay for Win. Suddenly the picture of Dr. Harris on that sofa was right in front of me, and I knew I hated him more than I had ever hated anyone in my whole life. I wished now I'd kicked him. And kicked him and kicked him, where it hurt.

And as I thought this I found I was beating my fists

173

against the kitchen wall and yelling and yelling. Then I picked up something—a pan of some kind—and flung it against the wall opposite, and after that I threw everything I could find, plates, pans, knives and forks, and then I ran into Aunt Jessie's bedroom and threw everything I could find there: all her china ornaments, her comb and brush and the plates she had on the wall—and every time one of them smashed and broke, it felt like something inside me was exploding. I remember Muff and Alexis tearing out of the room, and some small part of me knew that I was terrifying them and was sorry. But I couldn't stop, and I couldn't stop yelling.

After a while I realized somebody was pounding on the front door and that it had been going on for a while. And I heard voices yelling my name. I ran out into the hall, to make sure the chain was on. It was, but the door was open, and then a body came hurtling through, breaking the chain off the door, and there was David Haines and behind him The Sludge and behind him the super with his ring of keys. And Alexis, terrified, was running out the door and into the hall towards the stairs.

"Alexis!" I screamed. "Come back. They'll kill you!"

"Jesus! That's a white rat," David said.

But I was being held by him as I kicked and fought.

"Alexis! You've got to get him!"

The Sludge had me by the shoulders. "Alan, Alan, it's okay. Calm down. We'll get him."

But it was too late. Alexis had gone.

Later, The Sludge, David and I were in the sitting room. At some point, after I knew that Alexis had gone for good, I stopped yelling and started crying. The Sludge tried to say something, but after a while he just put his arms around me and held me and told me to cry it out. Which I did, until there was nothing left. Then I told him everything, Aunt Jessie dying, Muff getting sick, Winchester's being knocked down and finally about Dr. Harris and the money I took. But of course he knew about that. That was why he and David had come over and, when they couldn't get an answer, gotten hold of the super. "We've known something was wrong for a while," The Sludge said, "but we didn't want to seem to interfere with your aunt's way of doing things. I wish now we had interfered. But, Alan, why in the name of everything didn't you let us know?"

"Because you would have had the pound come here and take the animals away and gas them, the way they did in Detroit, after I told them Aunt Jessie was coming and we'd take them."

"No we wouldn't have. We'd have found some other solution, but I can see why you wouldn't know that."

"What's going to happen to them now?"

The Sludge looked at me. "I can't, in all conscience, leave you here alone any longer. I'm sorry, Alan, but those are the realities of life. You can come and stay with us for a while, until you know what you want to do, I mean if there's a relative you want to stay with."

"I don't have any more."

"Well—we'll work something out."

"The animals?"

There was a silence.

"You're going to kill them, aren't you?"

"No. I've promised you we won't, and I'll keep that. I'd let them come with you except for one thing. We live in an apartment. If we had an attic—but we don't. More realities. And my wife suffers from asthma."

"You have a dog. I know you do."

"Yes. We have a poodle, and the reason it's a poodle is that it is the only kind of dog—and the only animal—my wife can share quarters with. Poodles' fur is less like fur and more like hair—human hair—than any other animal's. That's why they have to be clipped. They don't shed."

"So I can't take them. I can't even take Winchester."

"No. I'm sorry. But I've seen my wife have asthma attacks and they are frightening. I can't subject her to them. But I've promised you, we'll find homes for them."

"Alexis is gone," I said. I felt terrible.

"Yes. I'm sorry."

In the end he let me stay there for another night and David stayed with me, sleeping in Aunt Jessie's bed. The next morning, Mrs. Gerbil had her babies. They were all born without their sweaters, that is, without fur. After watching them for a while David said he'd take them and I could come and visit them. His mother, he said, liked anything around that was having children.

Betsy took Muff and Wallace, and told me I could come any time and see them. After everything was put in storage and I moved to the Laurences' I thought a lot about Winchester and Alexis—Alexis, who'd been with me since he was a baby and trusted dogs, cats and humans and didn't even begin to know how to take care of himself. When I couldn't stand thinking about him any longer, I worried about Winchester. Every day when I called and asked how he was I felt worse, because he would be expecting me to come and take him home. It was then I thought about running away with him when he was well enough to leave Dr. Sanders's. The more I considered that, the better I liked it.

It wasn't that the Laurences weren't being nice. They were. They gave me a room to myself and even got a second-hand television for me. If it hadn't been for the animals, it would have been no worse than Aunt Jessie and Uncle Ian and all the other cousins and aunts I'd stayed with.

But even though I liked the idea of running away, I knew that I probably wouldn't get away with it. I was too young. If I'd just been three years older I could have swung it. But a kid is a kid and is easily spotted by the police. As I said, children don't have any rights. Like old people. And at that I thought about Mr. Lin. I stood there, at the window of my room, thinking about him for a few minutes. Then, before I got too scared, I left and went to the park. I knew it was about the time he'd be there.

Mr. Lin was there, sitting on his usual bench, and Ming was sitting near his feet. I stopped for a minute and watched them. Mr. Lin looked up. "Hello, Alan," he said.

"I'm sorry I left you that day. I shouldn't have. And I'm sorry, truly sorry, Ming got hurt."

"It's all right. Ming is recovered. You didn't know. Don't let it worry you. After all, for the one day you weren't there, there were so many days you were."

"But I wasn't there the day the gang came."

"You didn't know they were coming or you wouldn't have left."

Somehow, his being so nice about it made me feel worse. "Did you hear what happened?" I said after a minute.

He shifted his cane and folded his hands on it. "Yes. I'm sorry about that. It must have been very hard for you."

I was finding it difficult to swallow. The Sludge had cashed Mr. Rosenfeld's check for me so I could return the collection money right away. Then he told me he was not going to take me to juvenile hall about the money, that I had been under what he called severe pressure and he didn't think I was a thief. But that no matter what the reason, stealing was wrong. Only the next time to let people know I needed help.

"I don't really get along with people," I'd said. And I thought about Dr. Harris.

"I know that. You're going to have to learn to, Alan. It will take courage, but I think you have a lot of that."

"David thinks I'm a coward."

"That's not what he said to me. He said he thought you had a lot of guts and I agreed with him. After all, your animals were your friends, and you were laying yourself out in every direction for them."

Now I knew what he meant, because I was going to ask Mr. Lin to take Winchester. I could feel my stammer coming on, but somehow I got it out. "You s-see, Mrs. L-Laurence has asthma. B-Betsy has Muff and Wallace, and David has Mr. and M-Mrs. Gerbil. And the babies. But I could train Winchester to be a watch d-dog to look after you and Ming. For real. And I'd come and exercise him every morning and evening. Please."

"All right," he said quite calmly. "I'll take Winchester. It will give me a new interest. And it will be an incentive for you to come to the park with us."

So, when Win was well, I took him to Mr. Lin's, played with him for a while and left. I was grateful to Mr. Lin, and I knew I'd see Win every day, but as I walked home I knew I was without any animals now, and I hated it.

Things went on. Nothing was very interesting. I went to see all the animals, but as David and Betsy and even Mr. Lin were talking about them, I saw that they weren't mine anymore. The Kingdom had gone.

It was on a Saturday afternoon that the bell in the Laurences' apartment rang. They were out, so I went to the door. There stood the super from my old apartment with a small carton in his hand.

"I got your white rat," he said. "He was in the basement. Here." And he thrust the carton at me.

After he'd gone, I sat down and played with Alexis in my room, trying not to think about Mrs. Laurence having an asthma attack. He was thin and dirty, but I knew that as soon as he had some food he'd clean up in no time. He ran straight up my arm and nestled down on my shoulder and nibbled my ear. I was sitting there, with him, when the Laurences came home, bringing The Sludge's assistant pastor with them. They'd all been to some kind of a meeting.

"Alan—" The Sludge said, as soon as he saw Alexis, "I can't—"

"Yes, I know," I said. "Just give me time until I can find a home."

In the end, the assistant took him. "Nifty," he said, picking Alexis up and looking at him. "I used to be a psych major and had a white rat of my own. I named him St. Augustine."

The Sludge kind of winced. "Why?"

"I dunno." The assistant put Alexis on his arm and he promptly ran up it. "I thought he had the makings of a bishop in him."

About two weeks later The Sludge said, "A lot of city and state agencies are involved in your fate, where you're going to live, not to mention the British consulate. It seems you have dual citizenship. But they have confirmed that you have no more relatives, or relatives who seem able to take you." He paused and looked at me for a minute. "There's your second cousin in St. Louis, the one you told them you once lived with but who married and couldn't have you afterwards, so that you had to return to Scotland. Apparently the agency got in touch with her, but she and her husband now have three children of their own, and say they don't have enough room as it is. So that lets them out." Mr. Laurence stopped again and looked at me closely. "Is that bothering you?"

I shook my head. "It did then, when I was seven. I'd sort of thought they'd be my permanent family. But not now."

He didn't say anything and I didn't either. To be truthful, I didn't much care. Somewhere, dimly, I knew he and Mrs. Laurence were being nice. But with the animals gone nothing was real. Once—but I had made up my mind never to think about Dr. Harris.

"I know," The Sludge said slowly, "that you're not very happy. And it's very much too bad that we can't live with any animals except Pedro here."

I looked at their big gray poodle, whom I had ignored since I had gone to live there. At least he wasn't clipped like a yew hedge back in England, the way so many poodles were. But I've never really liked pedigreed dogs as much as I do mutts. And poodles always seemed to me the most pedigreed of all. And besides that, I'd resented the fact that Pedro was there and my animals weren't.

"I'm sorry you don't seem to like him," The Sludge said. "He's tried to be friendly."

"It's not that." I tried to explain how I felt about high-bred dogs. "I mean they're valuable. Like property. That's why people like them."

"Not necessarily. That's not exactly fair. We have Pedro because that's the only animal we can have. But he's still a dog, and we have him because we love him, not because he has papers."

"Okay. I'm sorry. And thanks for saying I can live here." I tried to sound grateful, because I knew I ought to feel that way, but didn't.

"No need for thanks. We're not being noble. We like having you."

He fiddled around with his books for a minute. "Do you have any idea what you might want to do when you grow up, Alan?"

"Yes. I'm going to be a vet."

The Sludge smiled a little. "Somehow I suspected that. Speaking of vets, your friend Dr. Harris is back. He put himself in a rehabilitation place and is busy going to AA meetings. He's trying very hard to be sober."

I felt the anger again, hot against the cold, which was all I'd been feeling since the night The Sludge and David broke in and the animals had to go. "He's not my friend."

The Sludge didn't say anything for a minute. Then,

"Alcoholism's a disease, you know. Like diabetes. You wouldn't blame somebody for having a diabetic attack. Do you know what diabetes is?"

"Yes. Uncle Ian had it. And it's not the same. It wasn't his fault."

"My brother had it—diabetes—in fact, he died of it. It was because of him and because he died that I changed careers and am doing this work. Only, he did it first and better. He was wonderful with people. But to get back to Dr. Harris—it's not his fault in the sense that you mean it. Truly, Alan. I know he hurt you, but try—try not to be so unforgiving."

I looked at him. "You're always saying I should like people. Well—I liked him. In fact, I even thought I'd like to live with him and help him with the animals and train part of the way to be a vet there."

"He was probably very fond of you. Must have been, from what you tell me. And he did a lot for you, Alan. For you and Muff."

"It's not the same," I said, and left the room.

It was a few weeks later and somehow they must have found out that it was my birthday. When I got home from school there was a big carton with a red ribbon around it and my name on it. I opened the carton and took out a very small, round black poodle puppy.

"His mother died, Alan," The Sludge said, "so you're going to have to take extra-good care of him."

I knew they were trying to get me involved with

the puppy. And I saw to it that it got fed and so on, but I didn't like it. At night it cried and tried to get up on my bed, but I wouldn't let it. I knew it would grow into a pedigreed black poodle, but I wanted Winchester, with his flying bassett ears and hound body and long tail.

Finally one night The Sludge came into my room. He was in his pajamas and I could see he was in a bad mood. I was awake because the puppy was crying and I was lying there, not getting out of bed.

"Can't you stop that dog crying?" he asked. "Nobody can get any sleep. Have a little consideration for others, if you can't have for the dog. If you dislike it that much I'll take it to a pet store tomorrow. Somebody can buy it who wants it."

"It's too young to be in a pet store."

"That's too bad. I'm too old to go without sleep."

After a while I got up and took the puppy back to bed with me. It stopped crying immediately and snuggled against my side. Then it wet the bed. Good, I thought. Mrs. Laurence will make a fuss in the morning and they'll take it back to where they got it. Then I remembered that its mother had died. Then I went to sleep.

Mrs. Laurence didn't make a fuss. She just said, "I think I'll get you a rubber sheet until you have the puppy trained. What are you going to name it?"

"I haven't thought," I said. "I just call it Puppy."

After a couple more days she came into my room and closed the door. "Do you have a name for it yet?"

"No."

"All right. I've been thinking that it was a mistake to try and make you care for it. I believe I've found a home for it. I'll take it there if you want me to."

I didn't say anything. Puppy had dragged my sneaker out of the closet and was trying to eat it. I opened my mouth to say yes. With a huge effort, Puppy picked up the sneaker, which was nearly twice as long as itself, and staggered over to me and put it down and barked. It was the first time it had barked.

"Well?" Mrs. Laurence said.

"I guess not," I said after a minute.

"Then you're going to have to give it a name and take it to the vet for some shots."

I waited another few days, during which I again visited Wallace and Muff and Alexis and Mr. and Mrs. Gerbil and went on taking out Winchester every morning and evening. I had decided that I would now pretend they were only on loan and that, somehow, they'd all eventually come back and live with me and we'd be together again, and that they missed me now as much as I missed them.

But after I'd seen them I knew that—except for Winchester—it just wasn't true. Muff and Wallace were obviously as happy as they'd been before. I couldn't even get Muff to come over and say hello. I told myself that this was because she was really just a kitten, even though she'd been in heat and was practically ready to be spayed, and therefore couldn't be expected to remember what we'd gone through together. But it still bothered me.

Mrs. Gerbil was pregnant again. When I put my hand in her cage she tried to hide under the wood shavings, and Mr. Gerbil just went on playing with a new ceramic toy Mrs. Haines had made for them in her handcraft class. Alexis had learned some brand new tricks, and sat on his new owner's shoulder and nibbled his ear.

But worst of all was Winchester, who was the same to me as he'd always been, except sadder. Every time I left he'd stand with his ears and brows up and whimper, as though he couldn't understand why I was leaving him. I thought about asking the Laurences again if I could have him, if I kept him in my room all the time, but I knew the answer to that. I thought about running away with him. But then we'd be caught and he wouldn't even have Mr. Lin—and they'd take him away to the pound. Mr. Lin, who saw the way Win and I looked, said one night, "Alan, I'm sorry. He's as happy here as he could be without you. Maybe someday in the future . . ." His voice trailed off. Then he went on, "I don't want you to have too much hope. But I don't want you to lose it altogether. Never lose hope completely. Strange things sometimes happen."

I thought about what he said, but it didn't make any sense to me. Then the next day the puppy coughed and threw up.

"Did you take him to the vet?" Mrs. Laurence said.

"No." I felt a bit ashamed.

"It's not fair to the dog not to. He could get distemper."

"Yes. I know. I'll take him."

On the way to Dr. Sanders's I started wondering again what name I was going to give the puppy, something I hadn't been thinking about for a few days. I was carrying him, but I passed a dime store on the way and stopped in and bought a red collar and leash. I put the collar on and attached the leash and Puppy pranced down the street ahead of me. I was still trying to think of a name.

I meant to turn off at One Hundred and Tenth Street. But I didn't. I kept on for another five blocks.

Dr. Harris's office was full of people. When he came out and saw me there he stopped and stared for a minute.

"Hello, Alan," he said.

"Hello."

"Can you wait a while?"

"Sure." It was Saturday. "Why not?"

When everybody had left I took Puppy into the examining room.

Dr. Harris put him on the table. I told him about Puppy coughing and throwing up. The doctor looked down his throat, felt him, took his temperature and let him play with a toy for a bit while he watched him. Then he said, "He seems okay. Probably just ate too fast. Puppies often do, and he's still pretty young. Hold him while I give him a shot."

When he'd finished he said, "What's his name?"

By this time I'd found one. "Ichabod," I said. "My aunt used to make me read the Bible to her, and she liked that name. She said it meant, 'The glory is departed.'"

He glanced at me. "Is that the way you're feeling?"

"Yes."

"I was going to get in touch with you. I wanted to say to you that I'm sorry. I know what happened and I'm sorry—sorrier than I think I can make you believe."

"Well, The Sludge says it isn't your fault. It's a disease."

"It is a disease. But as far as you're concerned, that doesn't make me feel any better—or any less ashamed." He looked at me again. "You're not looking very happy. In fact, you seem pretty down."

I didn't say anything.

"What happened to the animals?"

I told him about Mrs. Laurence's asthma and who had the animals now. Then said, "I've been to see them a few times. They don't even remember me. Except Win. He remembers and looks hurt and puzzled every time I leave, and that's worse. Mr. Lin told me to hope that one day I could, maybe, have him back. But not to hope too much. Then he said, never to give up hope completely, strange things could happen. I don't know what he means."

After a minute I went on. "I was thinking about coming to live with you when—when it happened. If I could come here . . . It's too late for the other animals to be with me. But Win—" I couldn't keep the eagerness out of my voice.

"Well, as Mr. Lin says, don't hope too much." Dr. Harris must have seen something then in my face because he added, "But, again as Lin says, don't give up hope altogether. I know it's a hard lesson. But it's important. Not just as regards me. But because you can never be sure what might happen. But to be hopeful—and I know it takes guts—somehow seems to make better things happen than if you're not. Your experience so far hasn't been very good, but what might happen could be good, you know, as well as bad."

I wanted to say something, because he sounded anxious for me to understand, but all I could think of was that for me nothing had seemed to work out. So I just kept quiet.

"All I can cope with now," Dr. Harris went on, "is not drinking on a very day-to-day basis. And doing my job here. I can't complicate things more than that. But at some point, *if* I can stay sober, *if* the various authorities can be reassured enough by my staying clear and clean for a reasonable length of time to consider me as a foster parent, then maybe."

I looked up. "Can you do it?" My heart was beating.

"We have a saying—people like me who're trying to get off liquor—one day at a time. As I said, that's about all I can manage now. But one day at a time—I hope so." He smiled a little. "So you see, I, too, have to make myself be hopeful. If I'm not, I won't make it."

He paused. "There's another thing. Win'll be all right. He has his sad moments when you leave. He'll remember you from one visit to the next. But he's a dog, not a human. And sometimes that has its advantages. When you're not there he has Lin, and he has him more than he'd have you, because you'd be in school. And being a dog, he doesn't sit and brood because Lin's second best."

He put Ichabod on the floor. "Ichabod will need some more shots when he's a bit older. And Alan—he's a good little dog. Poodles are extremely sensitive and responsive. Very ready for love—both to give it and receive it. And nothing that's happened is his fault."

"No. I know." I bent down and ran my finger over the silky black head. Ichabod licked my finger, then started to chew it. We . . . we'll be okay," I said.

The doctor handed me the leash. "I wish you'd find him another name."

"I like Ichabod. It's different."

"It's different all right. Okay. Ichabod it is. You and Ichabod come back."

I snapped on the leash and stood up. Ichabod worried it for a bit, then picked it up in his mouth and ran out, dragging it behind him.

"We will," I said, and ran after him.

Then Ichabod and I walked home.

About the Author

ISABELLE HOLLAND was born in Basel, Switzerland, where her father, a Foreign Service officer, was Consul. When she was three years old the family moved to Guatemala City, Guatemala, and when she was seven they moved to England, near Liverpool. She came to the United States at the age of twenty to finish college at Tulane University, New Orleans. Since graduating from college, Miss Holland has worked in New York City, mainly in publishing. She is the author of several books, including CECILY, AMANDA'S CHOICE, THE MAN WITHOUT A FACE, HEADS YOU WIN, TAILS I LOSE and OF LOVE AND DEATH AND OTHER JOURNEYS.